The Shenanigans Series—Book Five

ANDREAS OERTEL

An imprint of
HERITAGE HOUSE PUBLISHING
Victoria | Vancouver | Calgary

Wandering Fox Books
An imprint of
Heritage House Publishing Company Ltd.
heritagehouse.ca

CATALOGUING INFORMATION AVAILABLE FROM
LIBRARY AND ARCHIVES CANADA

978-1-77203-239-0 (pbk)
978-1-77203-240-6 (epub)

Edited by Hayley Evans
Proofread by Kari Magnuson
Cover photographs: Thomas Eder/shutterstock.com (statue)
Jorgen McLeman/shutterstock.com (two boys)
Nowik Sylwia/shutterstock.com (girl)

The interior of this book was produced on 100% post-consumer recycled
paper, processed chlorine free, and printed with vegetable-based inks.

We acknowledge the financial support of the Government of Canada
through the Canada Book Fund (CBF) and the Canada Council for the Arts,
and the Province of British Columbia through the British Columbia
Arts Council and the Book Publishing Tax Credit.

22 21 20 19 18 1 2 3 4 5

Printed in Canada

This one's for the Bruces—
Bruce Klock and Bruce Webb

CHAPTER 1

IT WAS 3:30 in the morning, and we were about to break the law.

"We better hurry," Eric said. "The sun will be up in an hour."

I stopped staring at Smoke Lake and turned to the east, where a hint of pink was already visible on the horizon. We'd waited too long to sneak away from home, and now we didn't have much time left to conduct our criminal activities.

"Are you sure you still want to do this?" I mumbled.

"Well, yeah," Eric said, then quickly added, "This *was* your idea."

"But if we get caught . . . we've had it," I whispered.

I didn't need to whisper, by the way—there was no one around for kilometres—but it seemed like the proper way to communicate at the time.

"Don't worry," Eric said, trying to soothe my fears. "We'll be gone long before anyone shows up."

My best friend groped around for the insect repellent that was wedged near the front of the wagon—the wagon we'd been pulling behind our bikes for the past hour. He squeezed a quarter of the bottle in his hand, then smeared the stuff over his perspiring arms, legs, and face.

"What if they have security guards?" I asked, staring again at the dark lake.

Now, if it sounds like I was looking for an excuse to *not* do what we were planning to do, you're probably right. But if you recall our previous shenanigans, you can understand my concern. I mean, trouble really did seem to find us, like... like the mosquitos that were now covering my arms.

"It's a golf course, Cody," Eric said, poking me with the bug juice bottle. "It's not a bank."

I took the insect repellent from him and wiped some of the oily liquid on my skin. I tossed the container back into the wagon and resumed staring at the lake like a dummy.

Eric probably knew I wouldn't make the first move—so he did. He took a deep breath of humid August air and started unloading our gear.

I snapped out of it a moment later and helped him. Together, we shuffled the wetsuits and snorkelling gear from our cart and arranged everything near the fence. The fence marked the perimeter of the Smoke Lake Golf and Country Club. But lucky for us, the fence wasn't much of a barrier—just three strands of rusty barbed wire stapled to half-rotten posts.

The lights of a car suddenly came at us from down the highway. We both froze.

Eric's pale features lit up momentarily as the headlights swung across the field like searchlights. His blond hair was plastered with sweat against his forehead. The car continued to follow the bend in the road, heading away from Sultana, toward Pine Falls.

"That was close," Eric said, sweeping his wrist across his forehead like a windshield wiper blade.

I nodded; my throat was too dry to talk.

Eric put one hand on a fence post and vaulted over the top wire. While the mosquitoes droned around us in frustration, I passed him the gear—first our ugly wetsuits (ten dollars at a garage sale), then the flippers, masks, and snorkels, and finally the mesh goody bags for holding our treasure. I looked in the back of the wagon to make sure we didn't forget anything and followed Eric over the fence.

My eyes stung from sweat and insect repellent. "Let's see if we can get everything to the water in one trip," I said.

Eric scooped up as much as he could carry and headed across the fairway to Smoke Lake. We'd chosen the closest route from the fence to the lake, but we still had to cross fifty metres of mowed grass. I trailed behind him carrying the rest of the equipment, finally catching up to him at the edge of the lake, where he dropped what he was carrying.

"Yikes!" I said, glancing at my watch. "It's ten to four. Let's get in before we're spotted."

We took off our shoes and T-shirts, and then raced to get inside the wetsuits before the bugs could find our unprotected backs. The water would be warm enough near the top, but on the bottom, you needed a wetsuit. I read somewhere that even warm water would eventually suck the heat from your body, potentially causing hypothermia.

Once I was in my ill-fitting neoprene shell, I began to relax—but only a bit.

"Ahrrr," Eric grumbled. "I wish I could see what I'm doing." He was still fumbling with the zipper on the chest of his wetsuit jacket.

I knocked his hand out of the way. "Move your fingers and let me see." He'd pinched the zipper, and now it wasn't going up or down. "Forget about it," I said. "If you get cold, just pee in your wetsuit."

Eric considered my advice for a few seconds. "You know," he said, "that would probably work."

"That would *definitely* be gross," I said, reminding myself not to swim behind him, in case he did get cold.

We walked into the water carrying our flippers. It was easier putting them on wet. I watched Eric spit into his mask and rub saliva carefully around the lens. I know it sounds disgusting, but it stops the inside of the lens from fogging. I'm not sure why exactly, but it works. The thing is, Eric always took forever to prepare his mask. It was like his pre-snorkelling ritual or something.

I waited patiently and thought about how much easier all this would have been if Mr. Scolletti, the head greens-keeper, had just let us swim in the lake during the day. All we wanted was permission to recover some of the thousands of golf balls from the bottom. Smoke Lake was a huge water hazard for four of the holes on the golf course, and it swallowed up dozens of balls every day.

Last week, Eric and I had sat for three hours on the other side of the fairway, where the wagon and our bikes were now parked, watching ball after ball splash into the lake. We estimated that at least ten golf balls disappeared every hour. And we wanted them.

Well, to be honest, we couldn't care less about golf balls or golfing. Golf was for retired dentists. What we really wanted was the money for the balls. It didn't matter to us if we sold them, or if Scolletti paid us for each ball we recovered. We liked snorkelling and we wanted to make some money, and we thought our offer was good for everyone. That's why we couldn't believe his reaction. I could still see his narrow, pockmarked face in my mind. "He looks like an asteroid," Eric had said later.

Anyway, Scolletti told us he'd *never* let us swim in the lake, and if he ever found out we had, he'd prosecute us to the fullest extent of the law. We didn't know what that meant, but it didn't sound good.

"Are you coming or what?" Eric said, pulling me back to the present.

"Yeah, yeah," I said, "I'm just waiting for you to finish spreading gob on your goggles." I laughed and flicked on my Pelican dive light, making sure the powerful beam stayed under the water. Eric did the same with his Nautica light.

"Let's stay close to each other down there," I said.

Eric nodded.

We didn't know what to expect beneath the surface, and I wanted us to be close in case we ran into trouble. It would be easy to get tangled in weeds, cables, and irrigation hoses, especially in the dark.

I popped the snorkel into my mouth, took a deep breath, and slipped below the inky surface of Smoke Lake. It was always fun when Eric and I went swimming and snorkelling, but this was different. It was 4:00 in the morning, and we could see almost nothing beyond the beams of our lights. And did I mention we were breaking the law?

As soon as we went under, we began to see golf balls. They glowed like hundreds of tiny eyes as our light beams passed over them. First just a few balls here and there, then as we got deeper, more and more balls. And as fast as we could, we scooped them into our mesh goody bags, always being careful not to stir the fine bottom sediment.

A minute later, I rose to the surface and blew hard on my snorkel to clear it. I sucked in some fresh air and headed right back down.

The plan was working perfectly. *So far, anyway.*

After several minutes of collecting, I paused topside and waited for Eric. He emerged beside me a few seconds later—and just like he always did, he turned his head and cleared his snorkel so that the water blasted me right in the face. I didn't flinch or even bother looking away, since my mask covered half my face.

Eric spit his snorkel out and laughed. "This is awesome, Code!"

I nodded. "Yeah, there are thousands down there. Just like we figured."

"Let's go a bit deeper," he suggested. "We've cleaned up this area pretty good."

I nodded, replaced my snorkel, took a deep breath, and headed back down.

Sure enough, as we moved away from shore, the number of golf balls increased. We were now far beyond the reach of the telescopic ball-scoopers that golfers use to recover sunken balls. In a few areas, there were actually mounds of balls, as if they had been squirrelled away by some underwater creature. This was going to be easy-peasy money for Cody Lint and Eric Summers.

The only problem now was that Eric's dive cycles were taking longer. The deeper we went, the more time it took him to resurface for fresh air and then go back down again. I should explain that I can hold my breath longer than Eric can. I'm not bragging—well, maybe I am a bit—but for some reason I have a natural ability to hold my breath for a really long time.

I sensed Eric heading up for air again, so I did some quick math in my head. If we each pulled out four hundred balls and sold them for twenty-five cents each, we'd have—

Eric tapped my head to get my attention.

I looked up at him. *What?*

Aiming his dive light at his mouth, he removed his snorkel and showed me his white, grinning teeth. I laughed into my snorkel, bubbles gurgling all around my head. Eric was clearly having fun.

I grabbed twenty more balls and struggled for the surface. My bag, now filled with over two hundred golf balls, was getting pretty heavy, and hauling it to the surface was becoming exhausting. Plus, the bag kept hitting the silt-covered lake bottom, making a mess of the visibility. I had to keep swimming through these cloudy areas before I could resume collecting.

At the surface, I was contemplating one last trip down, when suddenly, off to my right, Eric's light flashed wildly through the water. A chill shot down my spine.

Something was wrong!

Eric popped out of the water three metres from me. With four frantic kicks, I was next to him. I grabbed his arm and pulled him close.

I spat out my snorkel. "What's wrong?" I demanded.

Eric ignored me. His mask was half-flooded, and he was shaking like he'd seen the creature from the Black Lagoon.

I wanted to hold him—to calm him down—but he was already kicking violently for land. I'm sure he would have set an Olympic record, but the bag wrapped around his wrist slowed him down.

I raced after Eric, setting an equally frantic pace. If something in the lake had spooked my friend, why should I stay behind to be eaten by it—right? I caught up with Eric as he scrambled up the bank nearour clothes.

"What's wrong?" I demanded, flopping my bag of golf balls down next to him on the grass. "What happened down there? Did you see something? Tell me!"

But he wouldn't even look at me. His head kept turning to the left, then to the right—his eyes darting all around. He was really scared!

The eastern sky brightened at an alarming rate, and I glanced at my wrist. It was 4:25. *Crap!* The sun would be up soon. We had to get out of there.

"What's going on, Eric?" I pleaded. "Tell me what happened. You're freaking me out."

"A body," he said, staring blankly at the horizon. "There's a body down there on the bottom."

"A what?" I knew what he'd said, but I didn't want to believe it.

"In the middle of the lake," he muttered, still looking off to the east, refusing to even look at the water. "Where it was the deepest. I saw a body."

"What—like just lying there?" I asked. It sounded like a stupid question, but I couldn't think straight, either.

"No." He shook his head. "It was wrapped in a blanket, or a carpet, or... or something."

I stared at Eric, not sure what to say.

"I'm not making it up, either," he said defensively. "I saw the feet sticking out." He untied his goody bag from his wrist. "Let's get out of here, Cody."

My head was spinning. How could there be a body in the lake? If there was a body in the lake, that meant that somebody had killed someone. People don't die of natural causes and end up at the bottom of Smoke Lake. This was too much for one night.

"Okay, let's go," I said. "It's getting really light out now, anyway."

I sat on the grass facing the lake and pulled off one of my flippers. Something in the water made me suddenly freeze. The middle of the lake was glowing like a streetlight in a thick fog.

I spun around. "Eric! Where's your dive light?"

"Right here..." His voice trailed off, and he looked at his wrist in disbelief. The strap was hanging in the air *without* the light attached to it.

We both knew what had happened. In his struggle to get to the surface, the strap broke and the light sank to the bottom. Now the Nautica's powerful LED bulbs were casting a spotlight straight up to the surface.

"Shoot!" Eric mumbled.

"We have to get it back," I said, speaking more to myself than to Eric. All our equipment had our initials on it. If someone found that dive light down there, they could easily figure out who owned it, and then we'd have to answer some tough questions. Plus, the stupid thing was expensive.

"Come on, Code, let's go," Eric pleaded. "Just forget about the dive light." His face was speckled with feeding mosquitoes, but he didn't seem to notice or care.

I looked over at our empty wagon, then at the lake, then at the sky. Finally, I turned to Eric. "You get everything put away, and by the time you're done, I'll be back with the light."

Eric seemed relieved that I didn't ask him to come too. He nodded and began gathering equipment.

I didn't like the idea of going back down alone—especially after what Eric claimed to have seen—but I couldn't risk our light being discovered. It was evidence the police could use to accuse us of trespassing and who knows what else. And with a fully charged battery, those LEDs could shine for days before fading. That was how I justified going back to get the light. But I think I also needed to know what Eric saw.

I slid down the muddy bank and began wedging my feet back into the flippers.

CHAPTER 2

"HEY, CODY!"

I was about to swim for the light when I heard Eric behind me.

"Take this."

I turned and looked at his outstretched hand. He was holding the Manta dive knife he normally had strapped to his leg. He'd never used it during a snorkelling swim, but Eric thought it made him look cool—"Like a Navy SEAL," he said. In the dim light of dawn, the knife looked pretty scary. I didn't think I needed it, and I was about to shake my head, but a part of me said, "Take it." So I did. It sounds stupid, but I felt safer just gripping the thick rubberized handle.

I swam on my back until I neared the middle. Then I rolled over and looked around. *Bingo!* Five metres ahead, the surface rippled eerily over the lost light. I had to hurry. As the night vanished, so would the glow in the water—which meant if I didn't find the light soon, I'd probably never find it. Unless... unless we came back again at night. But I sure didn't want to do that.

I kicked my way closer. Seconds later, I was floating over the light and whatever it was that had terrified my friend. *Here we go.*

I took several slow, deep breaths and dove below the surface. A metre down, I began to feel the water pressure building in my ears, so I pinched my nose and blew. My ears gave an equalizing squeak, and the annoying discomfort vanished. The beam from Eric's light drew me ever closer, like a moth to a streetlight. Seconds later, I saw Eric's light resting against a section of silt-covered irrigation pipe. The beam pointed to the surface at a sinister angle.

I drifted over to the light and picked it up. It was brighter than my dive light, so I jammed mine inside my wetsuit and hung onto Eric's.

Floating half a metre above the lake bottom, I wondered what to do next. I knew I should leave—Eric would be waiting—but I still wanted to know what he had seen. I mean, he must have seen *something.* Eric wasn't a liar.

I swam a circle around the spot where Eric's dive light had landed. Following the beam cast by my light— actually, *his* light—I nervously moved through the water. There were still plenty of golf balls, but nothing out of the ordinary—certainly no body. Oh, well, at least I'd tried to confirm Eric's story.

My lungs began to burn, badly needing air, when something off to the right caught my eye. I swung the light two metres over.

There it is! But what is it? I swam closer. Eric was right. There *was* something wrapped in a carpet. One more kick... closer now... Were those boots sticking out? Yikes! It *was* a body.

But wait! That doesn't look right!

My lungs were on fire now, so I kicked for the surface—I simply had to. As I gulped fresh air, I realized there was something weird about the feet I'd seen poking out of the carpet.

Excited now, I filled my lungs again and dove back down. I found the body quickly. Using the dive knife, I reached out and tapped a boot protruding from under the carpet. The steel blade made a *clang* sound that echoed all around me in the water. *Huh?* The unexpected impact of metal against metal sent a shockwave down my spine. Getting bolder, I swam even closer.

This time with the butt end of my knife, I struck the boot again. The same thing happened—a big, hollow *clang* vibrated through the lake. This thing that Eric thought was a body was actually a *statue* of a person. Nobody had been murdered. But still... what was it doing wrapped in a carpet at the bottom of Smoke Lake?

When I got to the surface again, I gasped. It was almost daylight! I had been so focused on my task that I had forgotten all about the time. The sun was rising fast, and slivers of gold were poking out on the horizon. I also noticed Eric, who was impatiently pacing on the grass in the distance.

Like a vampire terrified of being caught in the sun, I raced for the shore. My legs were rubber by the time I reached the muddy bank. Exhausted, I crawled back up on the grassy fairway and collapsed onto my stomach. When I caught my breath again, I sat up and took off my flippers.

Eric dropped to his knees beside me. "Did you get it, Cody?" His eyes surveyed my hands.

I lifted my arm, holding up the dive light. "Yeah..." I gasped. "I got it. And I have good news. No one's dead."

Eric froze. "For sure?"

"Guaranteed," I said. "I'll tell you more when we're out of here."

Eric nodded, grabbed my wrist, and pulled me from the wet grass. He took the dive lights and headed for the fence. With a flipper in each hand, I slogged behind him across the grass. I felt like I had just swum the English Channel.

Eric jumped the fence and turned around. "I think you can take the mask off now," he said, gesturing at my face.

I smiled weakly, peeled the mask from my head, and passed it over. "Give me a hand with the fence," I said.

Eric put a foot on the middle strand of wire and pulled up on the top wire, and I slipped through the gap. I felt safer—like less of a criminal—just being off the golf course property.

Eric already had his gear and all the golf balls stashed in the wagon, so it didn't take long for us to tuck my equipment away. I grabbed the handlebars of my bicycle and began manoeuvring the wagon for our getaway.

"Oh, no!" Eric said suddenly. "Look!"

I spun around and scanned the area he was pointing at. Instantly, I understood Eric's alarm. "Holy cadoodles!" I cried.

"Double cadoodles," Eric said.

We were staring at a well-beaten path between Smoke Lake and the fence. We had chosen the shortest route to the water to make it easier to lug our equipment. But those trips from the wagon to the lake had left a clear trail on the dewy grass. It looked like an army had marched across the golf course and disappeared into the lake.

"It may fluff up in a couple of hours," I said. "You know, when it warms up and dries."

"I hope that if a golfer sees that," Eric said, "they don't get suspicious and tell Scolletti." Eric mounted his bike and led the way back to the highway.

Eric was right. Scolletti wasn't stupid. If someone reported an unusual trail heading to the lake, he'd figure out pretty quick that we were responsible. Plus, I was sure we had left a mess of footprints in the wet clay at the edge of the water.

I followed Eric to the highway, then across the black-top and onto the trail that ran a parallel path through the bush and all the way to Sultana. The bush trail took longer and required more effort, but it kept us off the highway and out of sight. When we were sure we couldn't be seen by any vehicles, we stopped our bikes. We still had our wetsuits on, and we were both sweating like crazy under the neoprene.

"So, what was down there?" Eric asked.

"Buy me a pop and I'll tell you." Snorkelling always made us thirsty. There was something about sucking air through a tube that really dried out your throat. I figured Eric would be thirsty too.

He nodded and grinned.

We quickly peeled off the clammy neoprene and changed into our shorts and T-shirts. *Much better.*

We continued our journey toward Sultana, sticking to the trails. The highway would have been deserted at this hour, but why take a chance? We approached the River-crest Inn from the rear and tucked our bikes next to the giant garbage bin. Except for an old half-ton truck, the parking spots all around the building were empty. *Too early for normal people, I guess.*

Eric headed for the side of the building, where a drink machine sat on a concrete sidewalk that hugged the building on three sides. "The usual?" he said over his shoulder.

I nodded. My beverage of choice was Barq's Root Beer, and Eric's was Sprite.

I walked across the parking lot to the adjacent picnic area. I wanted to keep an eye on our equipment, but I didn't feel like sitting next to a stinky garbage bin. I sat down under a tree and watched Eric feed coins into the vending machine.

My mind began to wander, thinking about how one thing leads to another, and how you never knew if the end result would be good or bad. The discovery of a submerged statue was certainly interesting, but could we mind our own business and leave that mystery alone? Or would we, as per usual, get drawn into yet another adventure, ending up in a heap of trouble? Based on everything that had happened this summer, I figured we were in for a rough ride.

Eric found me beneath the pine tree and handed me a can. "Here's your *barf*," he said, making fun of my drink.

I took the can, cracked the tab, and took a long swallow. "Thanks," I said, then hiccupped.

Eric sat down beside me and studied his watch. "Ten after five."

"We're still good," I said.

Eric opened his drink and guzzled half the can. "As long as Rachel doesn't blab."

"She won't," I said, assuring him of his sister's loyalty.

The plan that had allowed us to escape Sultana in the middle of the night and go snorkelling on private property was a simple flip-flop scheme. But for the scheme to succeed, Rachel had to cover for us if anyone came looking for Eric and me. Anyway, here's how it worked: I had told my mom and dad that I was sleeping over at Eric's house. And at the same time, Eric had told his mom that the two of us were going to sleep in the tent in his backyard. But after supper, Rachel had seen us loading the wagon with snorkelling gear and became suspicious.

"What's going on?" she had demanded.

So we told her about our plan to sneak away in the middle of the night to recover golf balls from the country club.

In the end, all she said was, "You guys better not get caught, or I'll be in trouble too."

Eric's mom left for work at 7:00, so we figured that as long as we were back in the tent by 6:30, we'd be okay.

We sat in silence for several minutes, drinking our drinks and watching Creepy Calvin, the breakfast cook, stack empty milk cartons next to the back door. If calling him "creepy" sounds mean, let me explain. Imagine a movie where someone is about to turn into a zombie. Or picture a vampire with the ability to function during the daytime. Well, that's what Calvin Frippley looked like. But even aside from his bald head, see-through skin, and generally undead appearance, he was rude and creepy— really, really creepy. Seriously.

"So, it wasn't a body?" Eric asked, repeatedly snapping the pull tab on his Sprite.

"Well, yes and no," I said, trying to sound like Sherlock Holmes. "The object you observed beneath the waters of Smoke Lake was indeed a body." I watched Eric's eyes get bigger. "However, it was not a human body."

"Stop messing around!" Eric said. "Just tell me."

"It's a statue of someone."

"A statue?" Eric tried out the word. "What do you mean?"

"You know—a statue, a memorial, a monument. I think it's made of bronze."

I watched Eric flick the tab a few more times, trying hard to understand. "How do you know that?" he asked.

"Well, it looked like it was a coppery colour," I said, "but if it was made of gold, it would be worth millions. So I think it's bronze. Isn't that what statues are made of?"

"Why would a statue be at the bottom of Smoke Lake?" Eric asked. He didn't seem to want to talk about what it was made of anymore. "And *who* is it a statue of?"

I finished my root beer and said, "Those are good questions."

"Do you think it's worth anything?"

A third voice abruptly interrupted our discussion. "Is *what* worth anything?"

We spun around and saw a police officer standing behind us.

CHAPTER 3

"GOOD MORNING, CONSTABLE Murphy," Eric and I chimed together, trying hard not to sound too sarcastic.

Brad Murphy used to be married to Eric's mom's sister—making him an ex-uncle, I guess—and he was a cop. Well, he wasn't really a cop—not yet, at least. Brad was a special constable with the Royal Canadian Mounted Police. That didn't mean he was physically disabled, or handicapped, or anything like that. It meant he was a trainee—sort of a junior cop. Anyway, we didn't hear Constable Jerkface come up behind us.

Or did he sneak up on us on purpose?

We didn't particularly like Brad, in case you haven't noticed. Now, I can't report one specific thing that we didn't like about the guy—it's just that he gave off an overall bad vibe. In fact, he was such a jerk that we couldn't understand how he passed the interviews and got accepted as a police officer recruit. Don't get me wrong, everyone has the right to act like a jerk, but Brad was really abusing that privilege.

"What are you guys doing up at five in the morning?" Brad asked. He shoved his thumbs into his police-issue utility belt, giving us his favourite pose.

"Nothing," I said quickly—maybe too quickly.

He looked over at our wagon in the distance. We had draped two giant beach towels over our gear. There was no way he could see the golf balls hidden beneath.

Brad decided to demonstrate his sharp policing skills at this point. "Kind of early for a swim," he said, poking Eric's wet hair. "Isn't it?"

Eric looked like he was in shock. A bead of sweat raced down his forehead toward his ear. "We... we were just diving out at the trout pond," Eric finally said. "This is the best time to feed them and swim with them."

Wow! I was impressed. That was a great lie. We had swum in the stocked trout ponds before. It had been fun swimming around with the fish and feeding them stale bread from the dumpster. But we'd never go at five in the morning.

"Riiight," Brad said slowly. "The trout ponds." He looked at his wristwatch and then at our wagon next to the smelly garbage bin.

I nodded vigorously, confirming that my friend's lie was the truth.

"You hauled your stuff there and back," Brad asked suspiciously, "and *still* had time to dive with the fish?"

"We forgot the bread," I said, "so we came back."

"Then why are you guys still wet?"

"Well," I said, "we were hot, so we jumped in the trout pond anyway... to cool off."

"Yeah." Now it was Eric's turn to nod. "We're not going to go all the way out there for nothing. That would be stupid."

The back door of the restaurant opened again, and Creepy Calvin stepped outside. He scowled in our direction—probably mad that we had parked our bikes next to his dumpster—and heaved a bag of garbage into the bin. A draft caught the corner of one of our towels and flipped it back. Calvin had been about to head back inside the building, but then he glanced down at the wagon again. He seemed to freeze and stiffen. I guess he wasn't expecting to see hundreds of wet golf balls. *But did Brad see them too?*

Calvin snapped out of it, shot Brad a weird look, and quickly disappeared behind the door.

Just then, a car pulled off the highway and rolled to a stop in front of the restaurant. It was Brad's carpool ride to the police station in Pine Falls.

"I have to go to work," Brad said, "but I think we better talk about this later."

"Talk about what?" Eric said. "Swimming?"

Brad, being a super-cool almost-cop, didn't immediately know what to say to that.

We waited. After ten seconds went by, he took two fingers, pointed them at his eyes, and then aimed them down at us. And just in case we didn't get what that meant, he helpfully added, "I'll be watching you guys."

Ironically, we were the ones who watched him as he strutted to the minivan that would take him down the highway to Pine Falls.

Eric wiped his face. "That was close."

"What do you mean 'close'?" I said. "I think he saw the golf balls. And now he knows we weren't at the trout ponds."

"He doesn't care about the golf balls," Eric said. "I was worried that he heard us talking about the body— I mean, the statue. Then we'd have some real explaining to do."

I wasn't convinced by Eric's reasoning, so I said, "Didn't you see his face? He looked mad."

Eric laughed. "Of course he's mad. He has to carpool with Ms. Cross to work every day. He hates not having a car, and he hates that after ten years on the job he's *still* a special constable."

"He really is a grump, huh?"

Eric nodded. "Yeah, he likes to act like he's a real cop because they gave him a uniform, a flashlight, and some handcuffs. But the handcuffs aren't even metal."

"No?"

"No," Eric said. "They're those plastic cuffs that you put your hands into and tighten by pulling on one end."

"Huh," I said.

Eric snorted. "I bet he spends the day filing papers and mopping floors."

I wasn't sure what else to say on that subject, so I said, "Serves him right."

Eric continued trying to assure me that Brad (also known as Jerkface) wouldn't tell anyone about what he'd seen—I mean, if he'd even seen anything. Plus, Eric explained, Brad had never been very nice to Eric's aunt, so Eric's mom never spoke with Brad anyway.

"Okay," I said finally. "We better get back to your place and inside the tent, just in case your mom wants to check on us."

"Yeah," Eric said. "We might as well take a nap for six or seven hours."

"I don't think it's technically a nap when you sleep for seven hours."

Eric grinned. "When I sleep during the day, I always call it a nap."

We mounted our bikes and pedalled down the deserted streets to Eric's house. As quietly as we could, we rolled our bikes—and the wagon—behind the shed and crawled into the tent. It was warm inside, so we both just collapsed on top of our sleeping bags and closed our eyes.

But I couldn't fall asleep for a long time. All I could think about was that stupid statue. It was so weird. Why would someone make a statue and then dump it into a lake where nobody could ever see it? Did the person who made it dislike it when it was finished? Where did it come from? Did someone steal it? But who would steal a statue, take it to a golf course, and then sink it in a lake? It didn't make sense. *That's* what kept me awake.

I felt like the statue needed to be found—like it was a real person. I realize that sounds goofy, but it didn't seem right to leave it down there forever. These kinds of thoughts tumbled around in my head as I listened to Eric sleeping beside me. Finally, I decided we *had* to get the statue out of the lake.

After that, I fell into a deep sleep.

"Psst."

I tried to open my eyes, then gave up.

"Psst."

I felt a tug on my big toe.

"Cody, wake up." It was Rachel, Eric's twin sister.

I propped myself up on my elbows and squinted at the open tent flap. Rachel was on her knees, looking well rested and clean. I felt tired and sweaty.

"Hey," I croaked.

27

Eric grabbed a pillow, rolled onto his side, and pressed the pillow against his ear.

Rachel ignored her brother and said, "So... what happened last night? Did you find lots of golf balls? Was it scary snorkelling at night? Did anyone catch you?"

"Yes, yes, and yes," I said.

Rachel's face paled. "You got caught?"

She already knew that we were denied permission to swim for golf balls during the day, so I didn't have to tell her that part. But I did tell her everything else—how we snuck onto the country club property, how we snorkelled in the lake, and how we found the statue.

"Why on earth would someone hide a statue there?" she asked when I finished. "On the bottom of a lake?"

"It's pretty odd, isn't it?" I said, rubbing my eyes.

Rachel twisted her mouth and squinted in thought. "I thought you said you got caught too?"

"Sort of," I said. "When we got back to Sultana, we stopped to get a drink from the vending machine outside the Rivercrest."

Rachel nodded.

"Well," I continued, "while we were there—minding our business in the picnic area—Brad Murphy snuck up on us. And he may have overheard us talking about the statue."

"Uh-oh," Rachel moaned. "He's nasty."

It was my turn to nod.

"Do you think he saw the wagon, with all the golf balls?" she asked.

I shrugged. "We don't think so. But everything happened pretty fast."

Rachel slapped Eric's leg. "Get up! I know you're awake."

"I am not," Eric mumbled.

Rachel looked at me and said, "We have to hide those golf balls somewhere. You can't just leave them behind the shed."

"They're hidden," Eric grumbled.

"They're not hidden at all," Rachel said. "You guys just dragged the wagon behind the shed. I saw it there ten minutes ago. Anyone walking around the yard could see it too."

"She's right," I said. "We have to stash the golf balls somewhere else."

"Okay, okay," Eric said. "Just let me have a quick cat nap."

I looked at my watch. It was 10:15. We'd already been sleeping for hours.

"Come on," Rachel said to me. "I'll help you find room in the shed."

I crawled out of the tent and followed her to the aluminum garden shed. She unlatched the handle and wrestled it open. The doors screeched in protest as they slid along their rusty tracks. Inside, the shed was about as big as my bedroom, and except for a lawnmower and the usual garden tools, it was mostly empty.

"This is perfect," I said.

"I know, right?" She rolled the mower into the corner, making even more room. "Mom and Dad used to do all the gardening together. But now, Mom... Mom doesn't even come in here."

"That's good," I said. Then, realizing that might have sounded insensitive, because Eric and Rachel's dad had passed away, I added, "I mean, that your mom won't come in here."

Rachel gently touched the handle of a rake, as though she could still feel her dad's presence. "It's all right, Cody. I know what you meant." She sighed and leaned the rake against a wall, making sure she put it back exactly where it had been.

"Umm," I said, clearing my throat. "Do you want to see all the golf balls we found?"

She smiled at me. "Sure."

We left the shed and walked around to the rear of the building. I peeled back a beach towel, revealing the hundreds of balls. "Not a bad haul, huh?"

"Wow!" she said. "Look at them all." She ran her fingers over the dimpled balls, stopping and picking up a bright pink one.

I leaned over and watched her spin the golf ball. "That's a good one," I said. "No smiles."

"No *smiles*," she repeated. "What does that mean?"

"Oh, sorry. Some golf balls have dents on them, from the clubs hitting them. And those dents look like smiles— like a happy face." I found an older ball with a cut on it and showed her.

"And balls with . . . with smiles like this," she pointed at the golf ball I was holding, "are worth a lot less, I suppose."

I nodded. "A driving range might still use them," I said. "But I doubt a golfer would pay for a ball with a lot of smiles."

Rachel dug her fingers through the damp mass of golf balls, stopping to examine the yellow ones, the orange ones, and the ones with interesting company logos. "We should clean these," she said, "before my mom comes home."

I agreed that that was a good idea, so we dumped all the golf balls on the lawn and scrubbed them with a push broom and some environmentally friendly car-washing soap that Rachel found in the shed. We both worked frantically, because we didn't want any neighbours to see us. Plus, there was always the chance that Rachel and Eric's mom might come home early from work. Then we'd really have some explaining to do. Not that there was a logical way to explain why several hundred golf balls were scattered on the lawn.

It was almost noon by the time we gathered all the golf balls up again, collecting them in two plastic milk crates. The balls looked like new, and it was a shame to cover them, but we still hid them under an old tarp and dragged the crates to a corner of the shed.

Rachel put a plastic gas can in front of the boxes. "I don't think anyone will find them in here," she said.

"Yeah," I agreed, "they're hidden pretty well."

We both stood in the middle of the shed for a minute, not saying anything. Rachel kept looking around, like she was assessing the remaining available space.

"You know," she finally said, "there's actually a lot of room in here."

"I guess so," I said with a shrug.

"In fact, there's enough room here to hide something pretty big." Rachel stared hard at me for several seconds, then added, "Do you know what I mean?"

I nodded automatically, before realizing what she was getting at. "Yeah," I said grinning, "this is plenty of room." I'd already made up my mind that I wanted to recover the statue, but I sure didn't think my friends would want to get involved in another nutty nightmare.

"I mean," she said, "if we *were* to find something and then *had* to hide it for a while."

"Something like a statue?" I said.

"Something exactly like a statue," she said.

"The thing is," I said, "Eric was pretty freaked out—thinking it was a body, and all—so I doubt he'll want to go back there."

Just then, Eric appeared in the doorway of the shed. He looked sweaty, and his clothes were a wrinkled mess.

"Did you guys stash them in there?" he asked. He rubbed his still-puffy eyes and squinted into the dark space.

"Yeah, but we cleaned them up first," Rachel said.

"They look a lot better now," I added.

Eric nodded. "Cool. Maybe we'll get more money for them that way."

"I'd take anything for them," I said. "They make me nervous, and I just want to get rid of them."

Eric looked over his shoulder, then lowered his voice to a whisper. "You know, I've been thinking about that sunken statue. And I know you guys are going to argue with me, but I really think we should go back there and get it."

Rachel looked at me.

I looked at Rachel.

"I'm serious," Eric said. "I know it's just a stupid hunk of metal, and I know we've caused enough trouble this summer already, but I want to go back and get it. I really do. And I can't do it alone."

I guess he wasn't as freaked out as I thought he was.

Eric continued, "You're both probably thinking that it's not bothering anyone down there, and that we should just leave it alone, and so forth. But there's something fishy about that statue. It's wrapped up and hidden on the bottom of a lake. *Hidden*." He repeated the word for effect.

I said, "We were thinking the—"

Eric cut me off. "Bottom line, someone took that statue from somewhere and dumped it. And we should recover it and give it back to the owner. Who knows, maybe we'll even get a reward for returning it."

I nodded.

"Okay," Rachel said.

"Sure, it's kind of stupid to risk going back and—" Eric suddenly stopped talking. "Huh? Are you both actually agreeing with me?"

"Well, yeah," I said.

"We already decided that we had to go back and get the statue," Rachel added.

"Then why didn't you dummies say something right away?" Eric whined.

"You seemed to be on a roll," I said.

Rachel laughed.

"Ahrrr," Eric groaned. Then he turned around and headed for the house. "I'm getting something to eat."

Fifteen minutes later, we were in the house and eating the grilled cheese sandwiches Rachel made for us—they were really good, by the way. And while we enjoyed our lunch, we were also brainstorming ways to get rid of our illegal catch.

"I wonder what the quickest way is to sell hundreds of golf balls," I said.

"Maybe," Eric said between bites, "we could place an ad in the paper."

"We can't put an ad in the paper!" Rachel said, almost knocking over her chocolate milk. "That will draw Scolletti's attention for sure."

I suddenly had a better idea. "What if we asked a driving range—a driving range far from Sultana—if they wanted to buy used balls? They could then either sell them, or use them on the range."

"Perfect," Eric said. He turned to reach for the phone book on the counter, when the phone began to ring.

CHAPTER 4

WE ALL FROZE.

I mean, there was nothing unusual about the phone ringing; I just think we all had a bad feeling about this call.

Eric slowly took the cordless phone from the charger stand and pressed the talk button. "Hello?"

Rachel and I could tell from Eric's face that something was up.

"Turn on the speaker," she whispered to her brother.

Eric nodded. He pressed another button on the phone and placed the device on the table so we could all hear.

"I said, is this Eric Summers?" It was a male voice with an unfriendly tone—almost rude.

"Yeah, who's this?" Eric said, taking on an equally impolite tone.

The caller paused, then said, "You should stay away from the golf course—from Smoke Lake. It can be... a dangerous place."

Eric looked across the table at me and mouthed, "Scolletti?"

I shrugged, not sure who it was. The voice was a man's. No accent. No strange diction. Maybe it was Scolletti, or maybe it was some other guy. If Eric kept him talking, we might be able to identify him.

"I guess that's good to know," Eric said. "But I don't golf."

"I'm not talking about golfing," the caller said. "I'm talking about the property."

"But if I don't golf," Eric fired back, "why would I even go there?"

"And make sure your friend understands too," he said, sounding agitated.

"Who?" Eric asked, knowing he meant me.

"Your friend," he growled.

"Yeah, but which friend?" Eric said. "I'm a popular guy, and I have a lot of friends."

"I'm talking about Cody Lint."

"He's not my friend anymore," Eric said, grinning at Rachel and me. "He owes me four dollars and won't pay me back. But if you leave your name and number, I can get him to call you, if you want to give him a message."

Silence.

I thought he'd hung up, and I was about to say something, when he spoke again. "Listen to me, smart mouth," his voice hissed through the tiny speaker on the table.

"If I find out either of you punks has trespassed on that property, you'll wish you were never—"

Rachel switched off the phone.

We knew what the caller was going to say, so there was no reason to let him finish. And it felt kind of good to cut him off mid-sentence.

"Scolletti?" Eric asked again.

"That would make the most sense," I said. "But I'm not sure if that was him. The voice was kind of the same, yet different."

"Maybe he disguised it?" Rachel suggested.

"Yeah," Eric said. "Maybe he was talking through a rag or something?"

I shrugged.

"Or maybe he was pinching his nose?" Eric continued. "That's what I would do. It always works when I'm trying to prank you."

"What are you talking about?" I said. "That never fools me. You just sound like you have a cold."

"Really?"

"Yeah," I said. "Really."

"Anyway," Rachel said, getting us focused again, "whoever that was obviously knows you guys were there last night."

I nodded. "Yet he didn't call the cops. Instead, he decided to call some eighth graders and threaten them. Why would he do that?"

"Probably because he's guilty of something," Eric said.

"But what?" I said.

"Well, for one thing," Rachel said, "he's probably responsible for that statue being at the bottom of Smoke Lake."

"That's why we need to take it from him," Eric grumbled. "He's obviously done something illegal."

"This is getting out of hand fast," Rachel said. "I'm suddenly not so sure we should get the statue—not if some nut is already watching the place."

She was right, of course. That phone call should have scared us all into staying far away from the golf course—for good. But it didn't. I was more determined than ever to get the statue. I got out of the chair and paced back and forth in front of the stove. Eric's verbal duel with the mystery caller had gotten my adrenaline going. I suddenly felt like I had a lot of energy—like I could move a mountain, or a statue.

I stopped and looked at my friends. "Let's get the bronze tonight."

Eric grinned.

Rachel shook her head. "Are you kidding, Cody? This is a lot more serious than just trespassing. The guy on the phone sounded like he could be . . . big trouble."

Eric turned to his sister. "But so what? Look, Rachel, we've been in big trouble for most of the summer. But because we always do the right thing in the end, everything always works out. Admit it."

"Now *you* must be kidding!" she shot back. "If we use that logic, we can do the right thing right *now* and just call the police. Right?"

"No we can't," I said quickly. "We can't tell the police we trespassed, or that we stole a bunch of golf balls. And we certainly can't say there's a statue at the bottom of Smoke Lake."

Eric jumped in and said, "If we went to the cops now, we would either be laughed at or arrested."

Rachel shook her head some more, but I could tell she was coming around. "I don't like it. We only have one week of summer holidays left, and it would be nice if we could just stay out of trouble. For once!"

I realized she had a good point, so I kept my mouth shut. I also felt kind of dumb still pacing around the kitchen, so I sat down at the kitchen table again.

Eric softened his tone and said to his sister, "That statue has to be important to someone, Rachel. And we can return it to them. In one hour—tonight—we could sneak onto the golf course and get the statue out of the lake. Then, when we get it back to Sultana, we can take our time and figure out where it came from."

Rachel took a deep breath and let it out slowly. "Okay," she said finally, "but let's plan the whole thing carefully. I don't want to take any chances with whoever that nut was." She pointed at the phone again. "He sounded mean."

"You're right," I said to Rachel. "It was tricky enough getting the golf balls last night. Trying to haul a two-metre-long metal statue out of the lake is going to require some extra planning."

Eric found a pen and a piece of paper and pushed them across the table to me.

Rachel shook her head at Eric's laziness.

"What?" he asked. "Cody's printing is neater."

"Sure," she said.

Now that we had decided we would go back to Smoke Lake to get the statue, we had to figure out a way to do it. The way I saw it, we had two problems. First, we had to find the statue again—and that could take a long time, because we didn't have the beacon from the lost dive light to guide us anymore. Second, if we found the statue, we had to somehow get it to the wagon. And since we're on the subject of the wagon, I should explain that our wagon is *not* your typical little red wagon with plastic wheels. Our wagon is as big as my bed and can easily carry a refrigerator, with its thick rubber tires. And if a person were lying in the box, you'd never see them because of the thirty-centimetre-high sides.

But first we had to solve the problem of hauling the bronze out of the water and across fifty metres of grass.

My neighbour, Mr. Jelfs, had an old rowboat in his backyard, but just getting it onto Smoke Lake would be as complicated as getting the statue into a wobbly boat, so I crossed out the word *boat* on my paper.

"Can't we just tie a rope to it and drag it out along the bottom?" Rachel suggested.

Eric nodded. "The bottom *is* mostly slimy silt and mud. That might work."

I leaned back in my chair and thought about that. It was actually a logical way to get the statue out. And the only equipment we would need would be a rope—a really long rope.

"Suppose we do find Ironman down there again," Eric said. "And suppose we can pull him to shore. How are we going to get him to the wagon? That's a long walk with a hundred-kilogram chunk of metal—even for three people."

"Good point," I said. "If we drag that thing across the grass, it'll rip up the fairway like a plough. And then Scolletti will have all the trespassing evidence he needs."

We needed to load the statue onto something, move it across the grass, and then put it on our wagon.

"What about a sled?" Rachel wondered out loud. "You know—a toboggan. Do you think the statue will fit on that long wooden sled you have, Cody?"

I nodded. I was sure it would. In the winter, we used to pile six or seven people on it and race down the hill near the riverbank. I had always tried to time my climb back up so I could sit behind Rachel. Sure, she'd be wearing a thick snowsuit, but it was nice to put my arms around her waist and hold her tight as we bumped across the snow.

"—After supper," Eric said.

"What?" I tried to return to the present.

"I *said*, take the empty wagon with you. When you get home, throw the sled on it. Then bring both back here after supper." Eric sighed and pinched the bridge of his nose, like he was talking to a dummy.

"Oh, okay," I said. "Great." I quickly wrote down *sled*. Then, still flustered, I underlined it twice.

Real smooth, Cody.

When I got home, I immediately began scrounging around Dad's garage for rope. I couldn't find one super-long length, but I did find three different pieces—a tow-rope, a water ski rope, and an anchor line—and tied them all together to make an impressive, but ugly, hundred-metre length. I stuffed the rope inside my wetsuit and put it back on the wagon. Next, I fished the sled out of the rafters and put it on top of the gear already in the wagon.

We'd decided to go with the same story again—that Eric and I were going to camp out in Eric's backyard. That was easy-peasy for the two of us, but Rachel had more of a challenge. She would have to sneak out of the house at midnight and then slip back into her bedroom when we all returned.

After checking the wagon to make sure I didn't forget anything, I pulled it behind the garage. Then, walking to the back door of the house, I turned around several times to make sure the wagon was out of sight. Satisfied no one could see anything from the driveway, I went inside the house and began vacuuming the carpets and mopping the kitchen floor. Those were my chores for the day, and I made sure I did an extra good job. I didn't want an argument later when I asked to sleep over at Eric's again.

The whole time I was cleaning, my brain kept bouncing between thoughts of the sunken statue, Scolletti, and that mysterious phone call. I didn't know why the statue had gotten to me; I didn't even know if it depicted a man or a woman, or a boy or a girl. And we had no real evidence against Scolletti, but it sure felt like he had something to do with the statue being down there, and it sure felt like he didn't want anyone to find it ... ever.

Well, it was found now, and it was about to come out.

With my chores completed, I went upstairs, had a quick shower, and put on clean shorts and a clean T-shirt. My sleeping bag was already in the tent at Eric's, so I was pretty much ready to go. Now I just had to wait and hope my parents would be okay with me spending another night at Eric's.

After supper, when I finally mustered up the courage to ask if I could sleep over at Eric's again, they both said that was fine.

"But," Dad said, "you'll miss out on movie night."

"Sorry," I said. "I forgot it was Wednesday." Normally, once a week, we had a family movie night where we all watched a movie together and ate popcorn.

"Maybe I'll get to watch something *intelligent* for a change," Mom said with a laugh.

Dad groaned. "Oh, no!"

Mom nodded to herself and mumbled, "I'll finally get to watch a movie without killer robots, explosions, aliens, or zombies."

Dad reached out and playfully punched me. "Thanks for abandoning me, Cody. Looks like I'll be watching a melodrama with lots of talking and no car chases."

CHAPTER 5

"ALL SET?" RACHEL asked.

I nodded and hopped off my bike.

"You're late," Eric said. "Any complications?"

"Yeah, two," I said, pushing the bike—which was pulling the wagon—behind the shed.

"What happened?" Rachel asked.

"Well," I said, "it took forever for my mom and dad to get settled. I didn't want to risk leaving the yard with the wagon and sled and have them see me from one of the windows. But they both finally sat down to watch the news, so I said goodbye and made my escape."

"Oh," Rachel said, "that's not so bad."

"But then," I continued, "Brad cornered me when I crossed Pine Street."

"Really?" Eric said. "What'd Jerkface want?"

"Not much," I said. "He just wanted to know what *that* was for."

We all stood and stared at the sled sitting on the wagon. Rachel looked like she was going to be sick. I guess she figured there was no logical explanation for hauling around a winter sled in the middle of summer.

"What... what did you say?" she mumbled.

"I told him we needed it to get firewood from the bush for the fire pit."

"Did he buy that?" Eric asked.

I shrugged. "I don't think so."

"Nuts!" Rachel said. "Maybe we should cancel and forget—"

"But then," I said, "I explained that our wagon was too wide for the trail we were going to use, which was why we needed the sled."

"And...?" Eric said. "What did he say then?"

"Nothing," I said. "He just scowled and walked home."

"Hmmm," Rachel said, looking anxiously at the sled on the wagon.

"Don't worry about Brad," Eric said. "He's probably already forgotten about us."

"You know what would make me feel better?" Rachel said. "If we did what Cody said we were going to do."

Not sure exactly what that was, I said, "Remind me again what I said."

"I think we should go into the woods behind the Subtelnys' house and collect some twigs and branches. Then we can make a fire and sit around for a while."

"Good idea," I said.

The Subtelnys lived one street over, in the very last house, and where their backyard ended, the forest began. All we had to do was follow the trail beside the Subtelny house and we'd have access to all the branches we could carry.

"And if Jerkface does go for a walk," Eric said, "he'll see our fire and know we weren't trying to pull a fast one. Plus, we've got a lot of time to kill, anyway."

Rachel and I nodded. It was only 7:30, and we had to do something until it got dark enough to make our escape. So we dragged the sled across Birch Street, through the empty lot beside the Roberts' house, and into the pine forest beyond the Subtelnys. There were lots of dried branches scattered all over the place from a spring windstorm, and we were able to pile the sled high in twenty minutes.

When we got back to Eric and Rachel's yard again, we dumped the sled next to the fire pit.

"I can see this is going to be a s'more situation," Eric announced. "You guys get the fire going, and I'll scrounge up some marshmallows, chocolate bars, and Graham crackers."

Rachel, who was already piling twigs in the centre of the fire pit, paused to look up at her brother. "You're seriously going to eat s'mores?" she asked. "You just had supper like an hour ago!"

"Yeah, but I didn't have dessert," he shot back. "Did I?"

"You couldn't eat dessert," she said, striking a match on a stone. "You ate three plates of spaghetti!" She touched the dry kindling, and flames quickly engulfed the other branches.

Eric laughed and headed for the house.

I helped Rachel snap branches, and then we leaned them around the burning kindling, forming a teepee shape. The fire pit was surrounded by half a dozen thick logs cut into stumps. We wiggled three of the nicer pieces so they were out of the smoke's range and sat down to wait for Eric.

It was a warm, late summer evening, and no one was cold, but it was always fun to make a backyard fire. And as long as our fires didn't get ridiculously large, no one in Sultana seemed to care or complain.

Rachel took a quick look around the yard, then said, "You think we're doing the right thing?"

"Going back for the statue?" I said.

Rachel nodded.

I shrugged. "I know we have to break the law and trespass to get it. But getting it out of the lake still seems like the right thing to do."

She nodded again. "That's kind of how I look at it too."

I picked up our fire-poking stick—a broken paddle—and poked the fire.

Rachel continued, "I wouldn't even be bringing it up again if it weren't for all the other crazy things that have happened this summer."

"I know exactly what you mean," I said. "If we mess this up, or get caught, people aren't going to be happy. Everyone is going to think we're the biggest troublemakers in the province."

"Eric and I will be grounded forever."

I stopped poking the fire and said, "But I still want to get it."

"Then let's not get caught."

Eric returned to the fire pit and spread the s'more ingredients on top of a stump. He turned to Rachel and said, "I told Mom you were going to stay by the fire with us until it got dark."

"Okay," she said.

"She'll probably go to bed around 10:00," Eric continued, "so it might be good if you went in then too. She'll be less likely to worry if she thinks you're upstairs in bed."

"Okay," Rachel said again. "I'll sneak out of the house at exactly midnight, and we'll go."

Eric rubbed his hands together. "I love it when a plan comes together."

"Nothing has come together yet," I reminded him.

Rachel and I watched as Eric carefully roasted a marsh-mallow. The white mass was browning nicely on all sides, but then he became impatient and held it too close to the fire. It flared up and blackened a second later.

Eric laughed and said, "I had a feeling that one was going to be perfect."

Rachel and I giggled, because Eric had *never* made a s'more *without* a burned marshmallow.

Eric ignored our teasing and slid the puffy black lump onto a square of chocolate. He then sandwiched that mess between two Graham crackers and ate it. He had barely finished swallowing the first s'more when he started cooking a second.

"Just be patient this time," Rachel said.

I nodded. "Nice and easy."

"Yeah, yeah," Eric grumbled, rotating his stick slowly. "This one's going to be seriously awesome. You watch!"

Rachel and I watched the marshmallow catch fire a minute later.

"Rats!" Eric said.

Rachel grabbed the stick from her brother. "I can't watch you eat another lump of charcoal." She scraped the burned lump of sugar into the fire, harpooned another marshmallow, and carefully toasted it for Eric.

My mouth was watering as I watched her slip the puffy brown treat onto another piece of chocolate.

"Would you like me to make you one too?" she asked.

I nodded. "Please."

"You guys all set?" Rachel whispered.

"Yeah," Eric said. "Were you quiet leaving the house?"

"Like a church mouse," she said.

"What does that mean?" Eric said.

"Church mice are considered to be quieter than regular mice," I said helpfully.

Rachel grinned, her white teeth flashing in the night.

"Whatever," Eric said. "Let's go."

It was exactly midnight now, but we'd stuck to the plan. Rachel went inside the house when the sun set, and Eric and I crawled into our tent. We read comics using our flashlights for two hours, and then, just before 12:00, we slipped outside and waited for Rachel behind the shed.

My bike was already tied to the wagon, so we decided I would take the first shift pulling our gear.

Eric pushed his bike across the yard and onto the street. I followed him, pushing my bike, and Rachel brought up the rear, as she was assigned the responsibility of making sure nothing fell off the wagon. And that wagon did *not* roll very efficiently on the grass. In fact, I was huffing and puffing pretty good by the time I caught up to Eric on Birch Street.

Rachel rolled up beside me. "You want me to pull the wagon for a while, Cody?"

"It'll be okay now," I said. "The wagon rolls great on hard surfaces. Sultana should be deserted, so we can take the streets all the way to the main trail. Then maybe you or Eric can haul it for a while."

We retraced our route from the night before, following the bush trail all the way to the Smoke Lake Golf and Country Club. We stopped only once on the trail to drink some water and switch the wagon to Rachel's bike.

When Smoke Lake was in sight, we stopped and quietly surveyed the area for a long time, looking for anything that might indicate a trap. I didn't see any vehicles, flashlight beams, or glowing cigarettes in the distance. Eric rolled his bike to the fence, and Rachel and I nervously followed.

The mosquitoes from the nearby ponds swarmed us fast. I lowered my bike and groped around in the wagon for the insect repellent. I squirted a bunch of globs onto my arms and legs and then passed the bottle to Rachel.

"It's all those bananas Cody eats," Eric said, taking the bottle from Rachel. "Mosquitoes are attracted to the smell."

"I suppose I could shower once a month like you," I said, smearing around the last gob of repellent. "Then I'd have the same impenetrable barrier of filth on my skin."

We giggled nervously in the dark, and then with Rachel's help, we efficiently lined up our snorkelling gear by the fence.

Eric and Rachel hopped the fence, and I passed everything across to them. Rachel packed the equipment on the sled without help from us, and in less than a minute, we had the wagon unloaded and the sled loaded. Eric and I pulled our barge across the grass toward Smoke Lake, while Rachel patrolled the rear, still tasked with making sure nothing fell off. We couldn't risk dropping anything and having to waste time searching the fairway in the dark.

At the lake, Eric immediately struggled into his wetsuit. This part of the plan was pretty simple. Eric and I would swim out to the statue holding one end of the rope, while Rachel held onto the other end. Then, when we found the statue, we would tie the rope onto it, swim back to Rachel, and all three of us would pull it out together.

Like I said: a simple plan.

"You guys be careful down there," Rachel said.

Eric paid no attention to his sister. He was already slathering his mask with a healthy coating of spit.

"Don't worry," I said, zipping up my wetsuit, "we will."

We plodded down the bank and slipped into the water. Eric popped his snorkel into his mouth and led the way to the centre of Smoke Lake. Holding only our flashlights, we swam to the middle in only a few minutes. I slowed down near where I thought was the right area.

I spit out my snorkel. "How does this look?" I whispered.

Eric squinted at the shoreline of the lake around us. "Pretty close. Let's take a look." He took a couple of deep breaths and kicked for the bottom. I sucked in a lungful of air and dove after him.

I caught up to him near the bottom. The sediment we kicked up last night had settled, and we could see for two or three metres again. We dove what we thought was a grid pattern. For five metres we swam side by side, scanning the bottom, then we headed up to catch our breath. With our lungs filled again, we went down, turned right, and searched another five metres. We surfaced, dove, and turned right again for five metres. It was easier than collecting golf balls. I just had to stay clear of the rope Eric had tied to his wrist.

Twice we noticed the lake bottom getting shallower as it approached the shore, so we had to kick back to the middle and start again in a different direction. Our neat grid pattern quickly became a mess, so we abandoned it and relied on our instincts. If Rachel hadn't been keeping the rope taut, we wouldn't even have known which direction we had come from.

I was just starting to feel panicky when I suddenly saw something important—something really important. There, on the bottom, was a three-metre-wide swath free of golf balls. All we had to do now was follow the ball-free trail from the night before until it bumped into the statue.

At the surface getting air, Eric punched my shoulder to congratulate me.

Yup, I'm a genius.

He refilled his lungs and kicked enthusiastically for the bottom, heading for the statue. I followed him, and seconds later we were both hovering over our prize. We knuckle bumped and headed topside again.

I removed my snorkel and said, "Excellent. Okay, let's cut the carpet free from the statue. And then we'll tie the rope around its feet."

"No problem," Eric said, heading right back down again.

At the bottom, we tried to cut back the carpet carefully, so as not to disturb the fine sediment. But as soon as we touched the thing, years of accumulated silt bloomed from its surface. Our visibility instantly dropped to zero again.

Kneeling on the muddy bottom, I sensed Eric sawing through the ropes with his knife. His body jerked with each section of rope he sliced through. I peeled back the last flap of rug and frantically tied the rope around the exposed bronze boots. Eric headed up for another breath of air, but I was still good, so I stayed down.

I waved my arms over the statue's face, trying desperately to wave away the suspended grime. But that didn't help at all. In fact, it seemed like I was making the visibility worse, and somehow drawing in more cloudy water. I wanted to sneak a quick look at the statue's face—was it a man or a woman?—but now my lungs were beginning to twitch for fresh air.

Darn! I guess the answer to that question would have to wait.

Eric was suddenly beside me again, pulling me up and away from the statue. At the surface, he said, "Okay. We're all set."

I nodded, rolled onto my back, and kicked for the shore.

When I reached the muddy bank, Rachel stretched out her arm and offered me her hand. Exhausted, I grabbed her wrist and let her help me up to the fairway. "Thanks," I mumbled, always surprised by her strength.

Eric peeled off his mask and said, "Must be nice to have an assistant."

Rachel ignored her brother and started reeling in the rope. We took up positions behind her and helped. The rope tightened quickly, and then with only slightly more effort from us, we felt the statue move. It was heavy work pulling it in, but the slick silt and clay did seem to help lubricate the statue's trip along the bottom.

Rachel was in front of me, pulling steadily on the nylon rope. We quickly found a rhythm that allowed us to pull in unison, and the rope piled up behind us a metre at a time.

I grinned to myself. *Maybe we can get this done without any complications.*

Then everything stopped.

I turned back to look at Eric. *Why had he stopped pulling?*

My heart jumped. Eric *was* pulling. In fact, he was leaning back on the rope with all his weight, like the anchorman in a game of tug-of-war. I grabbed the rope and threw my body back too. Still, nothing happened.

"Rats!" I said, panting to catch my breath. "It must be caught on something."

"Let's try a different angle," Rachel said, walking to the right with the rope.

The three of us lined up again and pulled hard. The statue moved a bit, and then stopped with a thud that we could all feel through the rope. *Stuck again.* We moved to the left and tried the same strategy. This time, nothing happened.

"You guys wait here," Eric said, already climbing down the bank with his mask and fins, "and I'll go down and see if I can free it."

"We'll give you a bunch of slack," I said. "Then, when you think you've got it free, give the rope a couple of yanks, and Rachel and I will try and pull it in."

"Okay. I'll stay in the water and follow it all the way in. In case it gets stuck again." Eric sat in the mud, put on his flippers, and dipped below the surface.

Rachel and I sat on the grass beside each other and waited. We nervously tracked Eric as he moved away from us. When he stopped swimming, we knew he was over the statue. He disappeared below the surface, and seconds later, the water above him churned and rippled. *Poor Eric*, I thought. He must have been struggling like a wrestler to free the thing. We stood up to get a better view of the battle.

"It must be jammed up pretty good," Rachel said.

"If he doesn't free it fast," I said, "I'll jump in and give him a hand."

The slack in the rope was picked up suddenly, and the nylon jerked twice as Eric gave the signal. We pulled the rope tight and continued to bring it in. It was a million times harder without Eric, but we managed to bring it closer, centimetre by centimetre.

I glanced up and saw Eric's head pop out of the water. His snorkel cleared like a whale's blowhole, and he disappeared again.

After four metres of rope lay beside me, my arms burned from the effort and my hands felt raw and blistered. Poor Rachel. We should have brought gloves.

She was getting tired too. With each pull, it took her longer to reposition her hands for the next stroke. It had to be close now. I thought I could even see the glow of Eric's dive light.

Without warning, Rachel's leg slipped out from under her on the wet grass. She teetered for a split second on the edge of the fairway, a metre above the muddy bank. And then everything seemed to happen in slow motion.

She spun around to stop herself from falling and grabbed onto my arm. That threw me off balance and I fell backwards, kicking her other leg from beneath her. She held onto me, and together we careened off the grass and toppled down to the mud.

Splat!

The fall knocked the wind out of me. I didn't pass out, but it took me a second to catch my breath. Rachel was on top of me, her face almost touching mine. Bits of mud peppered her sweaty face, but she still looked prettier than any other girl in school.

"Sorry, Cody. I slipped," she said, smiling—her breath tickling my cheek. "Did I hurt you?"

"No. I'm fine." She didn't look convinced, so I added, "Honestly, I'm fine."

"What the heck are you guys doing?" That was Eric. He was standing in the water beside us.

"We slipped," Rachel said.

Eric laughed and shook his head. "Ironman's right behind me, and the path is clear the rest of the way."

Embarrassed, we both awkwardly got up and climbed onto the grass. Five minutes later, we had the statue up on the mud next to the lake. Then with Rachel and me pulling on the rope and Eric pushing, we hauled the statue up and onto the fairway, next to the sled.

Rachel dropped to her knees and examined the face. "I don't believe it," she said, wiping mud from the statue's eyes. She leaned in for a closer look. "I think it's a Native person—an Indigenous man."

CHAPTER 6

I CROUCHED BESIDE Rachel and studied the mud-smeared bronze. The entire surface was splattered with clay, weeds, and grass, but there was no mistaking the features. Looking up at us was a sixty- or seventy-year-old Indigenous man.

"What a great face!" Rachel whispered in awe.

She wasn't kidding. There was something astonishing about it, and I was pleased we'd decided to go back for it.

The face had those lines around the eyes that people get when they're happy all the time, or when they're always outside squinting at the sun. I think they're called "laugh lines" or "crow's feet."

Rachel gently ran her fingers down the nose and across the mouth, like a blind person getting to know a stranger. The nose was big, with a slight hook, and it suited the face perfectly. Rachel flicked a weed from the lips. The mouth was set firm—neither smiling nor frowning. And the jaw was raised and tilted to one side. He looked like a warrior, or an adventurer—a guy daring you to cross his bridge.

"Let's just get him out of here," Eric said. "We can check him out later."

Eric and I quickly stripped off our wetsuits and placed them on the bottom of the sled. Then all three of us rocked and twisted the statue on top of the wetsuits. The wooden planks groaned under the weight but held together. The bronze didn't wobble at all, so there was no point in strapping it down. The weight seemed to keep it in place.

We grabbed the rope and muscled our way across the fairway and back to the wagon. My fingers, already raw from pulling the statue through the water, now felt like they were wrapped around broken glass. At the fence, I scurried ahead of Eric and Rachel and pulled up on the lowest strand of barbed wire. A rusty staple popped off the nearest post with a *zing*, allowing me to yank the wire up to my chest.

Rachel scurried under the wire and Eric tossed her the rope. "Got it!" she announced. "Push!"

She leaned back on the rope while Eric dug his heels in and pushed. The sled jerked twice and slipped under the fence. I let go of the wire, and it rattled back into place.

As I crawled between the two top wires, something caught my eye. I twisted my head and looked back at the grass.

Oh, no! Not again!

There was a deep scratch in the grass, running from the lake to the fence. Under the night sky, it looked like someone had stretched a thick cable across the fairway.

"What the heck did that?" Eric asked. He was leaning on a fence post, following my stare.

"Look!" Rachel said, pointing at the statue.

I shuffled over to look at the bronze. At first I couldn't tell what she was pointing at, but then I saw it. The right arm of the statue was bent, and the elbow was resting just below the level of the sled's bottom. The elbow had scratched a groove in the grass all the way from Smoke Lake. No wonder it had been so hard to pull.

"Should we try and fix the grass?" Eric asked.

Rachel shook her head. "No, I don't think so. We'll just make more of a mess. Let's get out of here."

We slid the toboggan—with the statue still on it—onto the wagon, packed our gear on top of the bronze, and covered everything with three beach towels. The springs on the wagon were totally squished from all the weight, but we were pretty sure the tires could handle the load. If we were stopped or spotted by anyone, they'd see the towels, but there was no way they'd see the statue. Not that it mattered; I had a feeling that we wouldn't be able to keep it a secret for long. We had made such a mess of the grass that even a dummy could see something was up at Smoke Lake.

Eric tied his bike to the wagon, and with a push from Rachel and me to get him going, he headed for Sultana. Rachel and I hopped on our bikes and followed. Eric barely made it across the highway and into the woods before he had to stop for a break.

"This..." Eric gasped, "this is going to take... forever."

Rachel said, "There's no way we can get the statue all the way to Sultana tonight."

I looked down at my blistered hand. "Yeah," I said. "We're going to have to hide it along the trail somewhere, then come back for it later."

"I knew it would be hard work," Eric mumbled, "but not this hard. It's going to take days to haul it home."

"Unless," Rachel said, "we hooked up the wagon to an all-terrain vehicle—a quad."

"That's it, Rach!" Eric said. "If we could borrow an ATV, we could tie it to the wagon and have him home in an hour." He pointed at the statue.

"Mr. Jelfs?" I said.

"Mr. Jelfs," Rachel echoed.

"That's right," Eric said. "He has two of those ATV things—an old beater and a brand new one."

"He might let us use the old one," Rachel said, "if we had a good reason for needing it."

"I've seen him haul firewood with it," Eric said. "Maybe we could say we want to get more firewood."

"That could work," Rachel said. "I'm sure he's seen us messing around by the fire pit, burning all that brush. It makes sense that we'd run out and need some real wood."

"That's it!" Eric said.

"We'll ask if we can use his four-wheeler to get some proper firewood," I said. "There's that old logging area between here and Sultana. I'm sure we could find leftover logs there."

"Right," Eric said. "We could pack them on top of the wagon as we drag the statue to Sultana."

"Okay, that settles it," Rachel said. "Let's roll him off the trail somewhere and get back to town."

Eric and I nodded. But doing that was a lot harder than it sounded. The spruce trees in the area were all mature, with few branches near the bottom, so they didn't hide the wagon at all. This forced us to struggle and roll the heavy cart far off the trail. The wheels on the wagon sank deep in the soft forest floor, which made going twenty metres take forever.

When we were finally satisfied that our prize couldn't be seen by anyone on the trail, we all collapsed on our backs and tried to catch our breath. I ignored the pine needles and twigs poking my exposed skin, and I stared up at the summer sky with my friends. High above us, a gap in the dark trees revealed the Milky Way and its billions of twinkling stars. And just when I thought the night couldn't get any more amazing, a shooting star suddenly streaked across the sky. It was so bright that it looked like someone was trying to open the galaxy with a giant zipper.

"Wow!" Eric whispered. "Did you guys see that?"

I heard Rachel move beside me. "Look!" she said.

I propped myself on my elbow and looked at the statue, where she was pointing. The bronze head was exposed and appeared to be staring straight up at the sky too.

"I think he's happy to finally be out of the water," Rachel said.

"Imagine how happy he'll be when we get him home," I said. "Wherever that is."

Eric slowly got up. "And imagine how happy *I'll* be when I'm in my sleeping bag again."

"Okay, Rachel," I whispered, "good luck sneaking back into the house."

"Yeah, don't get caught," Eric added.

"Don't you guys have any faith in me?" she said with a grin.

We were back in Eric and Rachel's backyard again, standing beside the tent. The trip back to Sultana had been uneventful and took only an hour. Too tired to talk, we'd saved our energy for pedalling home down the dark trails.

Rachel slipped inside our tent and came out a minute later wearing her nightgown. "Now," she said, "if I get caught, I'll just say I couldn't sleep and that I wanted to get a glass of milk."

"That's not going to explain your sweaty, mud-splattered face, though," Eric said. "Make sure you clean up downstairs."

She said goodnight to us and padded across the grass to the kitchen door. Eric and I crawled into the dome tent and collapsed from exhaustion onto our sleeping bags—for the second night in a row.

CHAPTER 7

"GET UP!"

"Go away!" Eric said.

"Get up!" Rachel said again. "Mr. Jelfs said 'Yes.'"

"We're still sleeping," Eric griped. "And I don't care."

But I did care. I sat up and said, "The ATV? He'll let us use it?"

Rachel looked showered and well rested. She nodded. "Yeah, Code. I asked him myself fifteen minutes ago. I told him what you said—that we want to fetch some wood in our wagon for the fire pit."

"That's great," I said. "So . . . so when can we get it?"

Rachel laughed. "Are you guys deaf? I have it here now! It's right there." She pointed somewhere beside the tent. "Didn't you guys hear me pull up?"

That got Eric's attention, and he sat up too. "That means we can get the statue today."

"Yeah," Rachel said, "we can go right now, if you guys want."

Eric and I looked at each other.

I shrugged my shoulders. "I guess I'm ready," I said.

"So am I," Eric said. "But I still want to eat a few bowls of cereal first. You know, for energy."

Eric and I quickly washed the sleep and sweat and dirt from our faces at the outside tap. Then we went inside and wolfed down cereal and glasses of chocolate milk while Rachel watched.

"Is it hard to drive?" I asked her between mouthfuls of Cheerios.

"No, it's simple," she said. "Mr. Jelfs only had to show me once. He said it works the same as any motorcycle or car that has gears. You just have to get used to letting the clutch lever out slowly when you first take off. If you don't, it's kind of jerky. I'll show you guys when we get out of town. Then we can practise and take turns driving. It's fun."

"Cool!" Eric mumbled. "I can't wait."

Rachel seemed excited to get going too, so I resisted the urge to have a third bowl of cereal.

Outside again, Rachel quickly explained how to start the motor. "It has a battery, just like a car," she said. "So all you have to do is turn this key and press that green button." She turned the key and pressed the green button. The engine rumbled to life immediately.

Eric whooped and laughed. "Awesome, Rach!" He slapped her on the back and yelled, "Let's go!"

"We have to put those on first," she said, pointing at the three helmets sitting on the picnic table. "I *promised* Mr. Jelfs we'd wear them."

Before Eric could object to wearing a musty old helmet, I ran over to the picnic table and brought them all back. "Pick one," I said, giving Eric first choice.

He grabbed the metallic blue helmet with a white visor attached to the forehead. Rachel took the purple helmet. And I squeezed my head into the remaining white helmet.

Rachel hopped on the seat and slid as close to the handlebars as she could. I climbed on next, tucking myself in behind her. Eric jumped on last, claiming the rest of the seat. Rachel looked over her shoulder, making sure we were all settled. She nodded her purple head, popped the machine into first gear, let out the clutch, and we were off.

Rachel made a wide turn on the lawn, drove across the street, and headed for the trails that would take us back to the statue. She was a quick learner, and it didn't take her long to get comfortable driving the off-road vehicle. And I was glad she was driving too. Knowing Eric, he would have raced the ATV all the way—and with three of us on the seat, that would have been a bone-jarring, helmet-bumping ride.

Thirty minutes later, we found the spot where we'd stashed the wagon. Not seeing anyone in the area, Eric and I jumped off the quad, making it easier for Rachel to back up into the bush. When she got as close as she dared, she turned off the motor. I helped Eric manoeuvre the wagon to the hitch, and then we tied everything together as best we could.

When we were all seated on the ATV again, Eric said, "So now what?"

"What?" I asked, startled. I'd been wondering if it was okay to put my arms on Rachel's waist. Some spots on the trail were a bit bumpy, and a person could fall off. *Seriously!*

Eric leaned sideways and looked at me. "So, we're just going to haul him to town and slip him into the shed?" He indicated the statue with a flick of his head.

"For now," I said.

Rachel's purple helmet nodded. "Then we can clean him up and figure out what to do next."

"I think we only have three options, anyway," I said. "We can keep it, we can sell it, or we can give it back to whoever lost it."

"Maybe no one lost it," Eric said.

"Someone has to own it," Rachel said.

"Yeah, but who?" Eric said, tugging the chinstrap on his helmet. "And what if they don't want it back?"

"That's what we'll have to find out," I said.

"Yeah, that's what we'll have to find out," Rachel said.

We decided not to take any chances with our cargo, and since Rachel was a careful driver, we let her drive back to the old logging area. We collected about ten two-metre-long logs and piled them on top of the bronze. It looked like the wagon was heaped with wood (which was great), when in fact there were just enough logs to conceal our metal friend. We tied down the logs down and slowly made our way home.

In the backyard again, Rachel reversed the ATV and backed the wagon right into the shed.

We untied the wood, stacked the logs next to the fire pit (we could saw them into pieces later), and slid the bronze onto the dirt floor of the shed.

"It's fantastic!" Rachel said, dropping to her knees beside the statue.

"He looks taller than he did underwater," Eric said.

I was still standing in the opening of the shed, wondering if I should close the door. I was nervous that the statue might be seen from the road, but if we closed the door, we wouldn't have enough light to really examine it.

"Come check him out, Code," Rachel said, inviting me closer.

Oh, heck! I left the door open, sat down beside Rachel and studied our treasure.

The statue was about two metres tall, but the bronze clothing made him seem a lot bigger. He was wearing some type of leather pants, which were tucked into boots. The boots themselves weren't like cowboy boots—they had more of a homemade look and came up almost to the knees. A winter likeness must have been intended, because he appeared to be wearing several layers of clothing, topped off with a jacket that went down to his thighs.

Both arms were bent slightly. His left was resting lightly on his belt. And the right arm—the one that had carved up the fairway—was bent at the elbow with the palm half-open and facing up. The way he was standing, he looked like he should be holding a compass in his hand.

The statue looked extremely cool: immense, powerful, intelligent, and maybe even friendly. I smiled. Bottom line, *we* now had the statue. And as they say in the movies, "possession is nine-tenths of the law"—or something like that, anyway.

Gazing at the statue, I wondered how we could find out where it had come from. I mean, why would someone go to all that trouble to make a bronze statue and then dump it in a lake? It didn't make sense.

On the other hand, if someone went to the trouble to steal the statue, why didn't they keep it or sell it? Why did they throw it away? Unless they found out they couldn't sell it, I suppose.

Rachel turned to me and said, "Let's clean him up."

I looked at my watch and nodded.

Eric looked at his watch too.

"What?" Rachel said. "You guys got something better to do?"

Eric said, "We're supposed to be at Clearwater Lake at noon."

"What's at Clearwater?" she asked, her fingers flicking mud from a groove around the statue's neck.

I explained that Mr. Provost, a cottager at the lake, had lost his wristwatch in the water at the end of his dock. He'd been messing around with the motor on his boat when the clasp snagged and broke. He'd complained to Dad about it a few days ago, and Dad mentioned that Eric and I had snorkel gear and might be able to help. Mr. Provost told my dad that he'd give us fifty dollars if we could find his watch—a fancy Rolex.

"Why don't you come with us, Rachel?" I suggested. "It shouldn't take long, and we can all go for a swim after." Sunset Beach was only a kilometre from Mr. Provost's place.

"Sure," she said. "That sounds good. But we still have time to shine him up."

Eric and I scrounged around the shed until we found a bottle of spray cleaner and some rags. Rachel was already enthusiastically knocking off dried chunks of dirt.

"I'll start with the head," I said, handing her a cloth. I gave the bronze face a blast of cleaner and passed the bottle to Rachel.

"And I'll start by getting some snacks," Eric said, leaving the shed. "We're not going to have time for a proper lunch later."

When Eric was gone, Rachel said, "I wonder how they make something this big?" She sprayed her rag and gently polished a shoulder, as though it were made of crystal and would shatter with too much pressure.

"I think they use wax and then melt the wax," I replied. I twisted the rag and wedged it into an eye socket to get out the crud.

"Wax?" she repeated. "How do you mean?"

I stopped what I was doing to explain. "Well, they make a sort of rough statue of the guy out of clay, trying to get his features more or less right." I paused and Rachel nodded. "Then they slap on a layer of wax and sculpt it the way they want the final statue to look."

"Okay, and then what?"

I had her full attention. "Then they cover the wax with another coat of clay. And finally—"

"They pour the liquid bronze between the two layers of clay and the wax melts," Rachel cut in, pleased that she'd followed the logic.

"Exactly. The wax melts, you break away the outer layer of clay, and you're left with a bronze statue." I rapped the chest for effect with my knuckles. *Ouch.*

"But what happens to the wax?"

"The wax drains out on the bottom. That's why it's called 'the lost wax method.'"

"You sure do know some weird stuff." She was teasing me now, laughing.

"I think I read that in a library book," I said. Then, to really impress her with my weirdness, I added, "The Chinese have been doing it that way for thousands of years. You know, making bronze Buddhas and stuff. Artists everywhere still do it that way."

Rachel nodded and continued wiping the statue. It was actually easy to clean. Most of the stuff just wiped off. And it wasn't damaged at all. Sure, there were a few scratches on the surface, but all in all, it probably looked the same as the day it was made.

"Hey, look at this, Cody." Rachel had been polishing the left leg, and now she pointed at the heel.

"Look at what?" I leaned forward, my head next to hers.

"This." Her hand touched the heel. "It looks like some sort of cover."

I bent closer, trying hard to see what she was pointing at. Then I saw it. "I think you're right."

Both heels had a brass plate on them that was about the size of a playing card. The plate was flush with the rest of the boot, and unless you knew it was there, you'd never see it.

"Maybe it comes off," she said, jumping up.

Rachel rummaged around in an old toolbox until she found a screwdriver and a hammer. She passed the screwdriver to me, and I pushed the flat edge of the screwdriver into one of the seams. I held the tool steady, and Rachel tapped it in with the hammer. I pried the screwdriver back.

Clang. The brass plate popped off and hit the floor.

I leaned forward to take a look, but Rachel's head was already investigating the opening.

"There's nothing in it," Rachel said, sounding disappointed, as though she thought it would be crammed with diamonds.

I peered inside too, and then felt around with my hand. "Well, I can feel two holes in the bottom of the boot—one at the ball of the foot, and one under the heel. I think the mounting bolts must go through the holes. And then they're tightened up from the inside through these openings in the heels."

"And then the covers get popped on again," she said.

"Yeah. I think so. I can't see any other purpose for the covers—or the holes."

Rachel picked the bronze plate off the floor and gave it to me. It was heavy for something so small. No wonder we had such a hard time hauling the statue out of the lake. I was about to tap the cover back into place when Rachel snatched it from my grasp.

"Wait!" she cried. Wiping the inside surface, she held it up for me to see. "There's writing on it."

Affixed to the bronze surface was a five-centimetre-square metal label. It said:

WESTERN CANADIAN BRONZE
Calgary, Alberta
No. MCC-04-28-0042

"Now we're getting somewhere," she said.

I agreed. "All we have to do now is phone Western Canadian Bronze and ask them who ordered this guy. Then we can call him or her and give it back. And like Eric always says, maybe we can even collect a reward."

"Let's call them now!" Rachel said. She was just as excited as I was.

"Okay," I said. "But you might have some explaining to do when your mom gets the phone bill."

Rachel sprang from the ground and took off for the house to get the cordless phone. I continued wiping down the statue, finishing just as Rachel returned.

"Eric's making us sandwiches," she said, passing me the phone. "You do the talking."

I dialled directory assistance for Alberta and waited. Rachel leaned over and pressed the speaker button on the phone so she could hear too.

"Welcome to Telus. Directory assistance for what city, please?" a female recording asked.

I held out the phone to Rachel. "Calgary," she said. I got a playful punch on the arm from her for putting her on the spot.

"For what listing?" It was a real person now—a male.

"For Western Canadian Bronze," I said.

"Western Canadian Bronze," he repeated. "I have no listing."

Rachel groaned.

"What about Canadian Bronze?" I asked.

"I have no listing for Canadian Bronze," he said, sounding kind of like a robot too.

"Can you look for any businesses that make bronze statues?" I was getting desperate.

"One moment, please." We heard the faint clicking of a computer keyboard as he searched. Five seconds later, he said, "I have 'Jerry's Genuine Bronze Trophies.'"

I was pretty sure we weren't looking for Jerry, so I thanked the operator and hung up.

"Oh, well, it was worth a try," I said.

"Maybe they went out of business or something," Rachel suggested.

"That's what I was thinking too," I said. "I'll search the Internet a bit when I get home."

Rachel took three lawn chairs down from hooks on the wall and passed them to me. I popped them open and placed them on the ground around the statue.

Rachel sat down and said, "He looks good."

I nodded and carefully sat on the brittle-looking nylon straps of my chair. "What about those numbers?" I wondered out loud.

"The ones on the label?" she said.

I extracted myself from the chair and looked at the identification tag again—the one inside the boot. "MCC, zero-four, two-eight, zero-zero-four-two," I said, reading the letters and numbers out loud. "Must be the identification of the statue."

"Or some kind of coding for a date."

"Could be," I said. "Like the day they cast it, or shipped it, or something like that."

"You know," Rachel said, "he could have been at the bottom of Smoke Lake for decades." She leaned back again, like she had to accept that herself.

"Now he's out." I sat down beside her again.

"Couldn't we just ask around town if someone lost a statue in the last five years, ten years, or fifty years?" she said.

I shook my head. "No, we can't. I don't think we should let anyone know we have it—at least, not yet. Someone went to a lot of trouble to hide him, and I wouldn't want that person to know we have him. Plus, if we told people we had it, they'd want to know *where* we got it. And then we'd be in deep trouble."

"Why? It's been sitting at the bottom of a lake. Isn't there some kind of a 'finders keepers' rule?"

"I don't think that rule applies," I said, "when you have to break the law to do the finding. Remember, Scolletti *specifically* told us we weren't to go there. We ignored him, we trespassed, and then we *stole* something from private property."

Rachel considered that for a minute, then said, "So we can't even say that we didn't know it was private property."

"That's right," I said. "And whether he's involved with this statue thing or not, I think Scolletti is mean enough to do it—to call the police on us."

"So what can we do, if we can't tell anyone?" she said, sounding frustrated.

"We'll have to snoop around on our own ... carefully."

"Like we always do, I guess."

At that moment, Eric walked in carrying a plate of sandwiches. He strolled over to the bronze and circled around it, never taking his eyes off the shiny surface—like he was checking out a used car. "You guys have been busy," he commented. "This is definitely an improvement."

He took a peanut butter and jam sandwich from the plate and passed the plate to me. Then he pointed to the brass cover I was still holding. "What d'you got there?" he asked between bites.

"Well, Mr. Summers," I said, doing my Sherlock Holmes bit again, "in your absence, and with the kind assistance of your sibling, we have deduced two things.

First, we have concluded, through detailed analysis, that the statue before us was cast by a company called Western Canadian Bronze."

Rachel laughed.

"Pray continue, Mr. Lint," Eric said, getting into the spirit.

"Second, we have further assessed the evidence and have come to the conclusion that this magnificent piece of art was produced in Calgary, Alberta, Canada."

"Really?" Eric looked astonished. "How could you possibly know that?"

CHAPTER 8

RACHEL AND I spent the next five minutes informing Eric about our discovery, and also about our unsuccessful phone call. If we didn't have the ID plate to show him, he wouldn't have believed a word of it—and who could blame him?

I reminded Eric about our promise to look for Mr. Provost's Rolex. "So maybe on the way back from Clearwater Lake," I said, "we can stop at my house and do some Googling."

Eric seemed to not hear me. He was standing over the statue, staring intensely down at the bronze face. Suddenly, he snapped his fingers. "That's it!" he cried.

Rachel jumped, startled. "What's 'it'?" she asked.

"The bronze," Eric said, pointing at the statue. "I thought there was something familiar about it this morning. But now that you guys have him cleaned up, it's more obvious."

I got up and stood next to Eric. "What's obvious?" I asked, looking down at the face.

"Well, maybe it's just me," Eric said, "but don't you guys think he looks a lot like Mr. Ghost-Keeper? You know, the elder we met five hundred years ago?"

Rachel came over and stood on the other side of her brother.

I squinted at the face, trying hard to recall the old storyteller we had met earlier that summer when we had accidentally time-travelled through a wormhole.

"He could be a descendant," Rachel finally said. "The nose, the mouth, the cheekbones—they really are very similar.

Eric nodded. "Yeah, I'm not saying this is *him*—Ghost-Keeper—but he sure looks a lot like him."

"It's certainly possible," I said, "that his features were passed on to his kids and grandkids. And he did live in the area."

"Wow!" Eric said. He pulled up a lawn chair and sat down. "This is almost like destiny or something."

"How do you figure that?" Rachel asked.

"Well," Eric said, "when we were stuck in the past, Ghost-Keeper and the Cree helped us get back here. And now we've stumbled upon this likeness of Ghost-Keeper, and we're going to help him get back to wherever he belongs."

Rachel looked at Eric and said, "That's a nice way to look at it, but the resemblance could also be a coincidence."

"We'll see," Eric said. "We'll see.

Ten minutes later, we were getting ready for our Clearwater Lake assignment. We crammed one wetsuit, one mask, and one set of flippers into a backpack. Then, before we left, we quickly covered the statue with an old tarp and closed the shed door.

We pedalled east out of town. When we crossed the bridge over the river, we spread out and rode side by side. Cars were infrequent, so it was okay to hog the road. We reviewed what we knew and what we didn't know. We knew who had made the statue, and where. And we knew it was a likeness of a North American Indigenous person—probably Cree, and possibly a descendant of our friend Ghost-Keeper. But we still didn't know who owned it, or why it had been dumped in Smoke Lake.

But that was all about to change with one clue. I just wish that clue hadn't included my family.

Mr. Provost lived on the south side of Clearwater Lake, a small lake three kilometres from Sultana. When we pulled into his paved driveway, I understood how he could afford an expensive Rolex. The house was a two-storey log cabin—built with real logs, not log siding—and it was massive. To call it a "cabin" was crazy. It was bigger than any house in Sultana.

Mr. Provost stood in the garage as we rolled to a stop. It looked like he was tinkering with a chainsaw. He was skinny, suntanned, and wearing only shorts. And he was really old—in his eighties for sure.

He turned from his workbench and eyed us with suspicion. The garage was doublewide and complete with "his" and "hers" signs swaying gently over each half. The "hers" vehicle was missing, and the "his" was a red sport utility vehicle. The far wall was stacked with newspapers all the way up to the roof; I had never seen so many in one place.

We dropped our bikes and approached the garage.

Mr. Provost dropped his screwdriver on the bench without taking his eyes off of us. It reminded me of a Wild West showdown. I could just imagine what he was thinking: *Crazy teenagers, what the heck do they want?*

"Hi, Mr. Provost," I said, thinking I'd better break the ice before he got his shotgun. "I'm Cody. You mentioned to my dad that you lost your watch."

No response.

"You told him that you dropped your wristwatch in the lake?" I tried again—louder this time. He could be hard of hearing, like most old people. "You wanted us to find it?"

Still nothing.

Never mind deaf, maybe he is Alzheimering.

"Ohhh," he said, realizing at last that we weren't there to steal his lawn ornaments. "I'm sorry. Please forgive my manners. I was expecting someone much older. You kids look too young to be divers."

I quickly explained that we would be snorkelling, not scuba diving. Then I introduced Eric and Rachel, and everyone shook hands. He cheered up even more when Rachel said he had a beautiful place. Grabbing her hand, he led us around the yard like a tour guide. The tour ended at his dock—a dock that seemed more like a public marina.

The lake was called Clearwater for a good reason. On a sunny day, the visibility underwater was five metres. And on a lousy day, you could probably still see farther than in any other lake in the area. The local lodge operator proudly told tourists that it was one of the three clearest lakes in the world. I'm not sure if that's true, but believe me, it was pretty clear—and super cold.

Standing at the end of Mr. Provost's dock, I knew today was a good snorkelling day. Only the slightest ripple tickled the surface of the lake, and the water was a great colour—nothing but blue. Greys and greens often meant waves had stirred up the bottom, making a mess of the visibility.

"Perfect," Eric said, reading my mind.

I nodded. "Where did you lose the watch, Mr. Provost?" He was pointing out a small lake trout to Rachel, at the side of the dock. He didn't seem all that interested in finding his Rolex.

"Huh? Oh, right, the watch." He walked over to the end of the dock, stuck his arm straight out and pointed down with his thumb. "If a fish didn't take it, it's here."

Eric and I looked at each other, and I knew we were both thinking the same thing. *Yeah, right.* When someone says the *exact location* they lost anything, you have to be suspicious.

"How deep is it here, sir?" Eric asked, staring over the edge.

"Four metres." He turned to Rachel. "Come on up to the house. We'll have some lemonade. Let's let the boys work." He grinned at us like it was all a practical joke and started back down the dock toward his mansion.

Rachel shrugged her shoulders and followed him.

When they were gone, I turned to Eric. "Well, how do you want to do this?"

Eric said, "Just do your thing."

Doing "my thing" was holding my breath (also known as freediving). And like I said earlier, I was getting really good at it. "Yeah," I said, "that's what I was thinking."

There was no point in Eric going down, because we both knew I could hold my breath twice as long as he could. My record of two minutes and ten seconds wasn't even close to the fifteen-minute times professional free-divers were capable of, but still, I was pleased with my unique ability to stay underwater for a long time.

"But what if he's wrong," I said, continuing to gripe, "and it's not right here? Or what if he's senile and only *thinks* he dropped it here? Or what if a—"

"A fish ate it?" Eric interrupted. "Just hurry up so we can go to the beach. I want to cool off."

"Then maybe *you* should get in the water and find the watch."

"I'm hot and sweaty," Eric said, "not stupid."

"I hate to tell you, but the water at Sunset Beach is just as cold as it is here."

Eric laughed. "Okay, maybe I'm stupid. But you're still getting the watch. I'll be your helper."

I shook my head and chuckled. "And how will you assist me?"

"I'll be right here on the dock, catching some rays." Eric stretched out on the decking.

It took me less than five minutes to put on my still-damp wetsuit and slip on my flippers. Eric propped himself up on one elbow as I got ready to enter the water. He knew my entrance would be entertaining. Sure, I had a wetsuit on, but until my body warmed up that thin layer of water between the neoprene and me, I was going to be in pain.

"Don't dawdle while you're down there," Eric said gleefully. "I know it can be tempting to enjoy the spa-like water."

I stuck my flippered foot in the lake and it immediately went numb. I knew the wetsuit would do its job in a minute, but gosh that initial shock was horrible!

"Gimme a count, at least," I groaned.

Eric laughed, enjoying every second of my agony. "Five, four, three, two, one, go-go-go!"

I pushed myself into the icy water. I didn't have to swim anywhere, because I was right over the *exact* spot Mr. Provost had indicated. But I still kicked my legs and splashed around in a circle, trying to warm up. I dunked my head and grabbed onto the dock. Eric passed down my mask and snorkel, and I defogged it with some spit. He was sitting up now with his feet hanging over the edge, except his feet didn't reach the lake.

Floating with my face down, I concentrated on slowing down my heart rate. When I felt ready, I inhaled and exhaled rapidly three times—trying to purge the carbon dioxide from my blood. The theory was that this tricked your brain into not wanting your lungs to breathe, which meant you could stay down and free-dive longer. But you had to be careful too, because if you overdid the hyper-ventilation, your brain could forget to breathe altogether, and ... well, that's obviously not good.

I took a fourth deep breath and held it.

Jackknifing my body, I kicked my legs out of the water, letting my weight drive me to the bottom. Keeping one hand on my nose, I blew continuously to equalize the pressure that built up.

Now, when I said I could hold my breath for over two minutes, I was talking about warm water. There was no way could I do that in water this cold.

Anyway, the water was nice and clear, and I could see where I was all the way down. The steel post of the dock was two metres away, providing a nice reference point as I descended. When I reached the bottom, I began scanning the area. After my second spiral pattern, my lungs began to crave air. But I expected that and wasn't alarmed.

I continued looking for the watch. But where was the stupid thing? A silver watch should twinkle and sparkle and stick out like a ... like a ...

Whatever, Cody. Just hurry. I did another sweep of the area beside the dock. Nope. It just wasn't here. Time to go up.

Wait! Something shiny ... Wedged between those rocks ... It's not silver—it's gold! The watch is gold.

I grabbed the Rolex and kicked for the top—my brain threatening to pack it in. I exhaled all the way up, trying to relieve the pressure on my lungs. Shooting through the surface, I gasped hungrily for air.

I held my arms above my head and let Eric hoist me onto the dock. Then I flopped on the deck like a cooked noodle. Air had never tasted so good. I stayed on my back, letting my wetsuit absorb the heat from the sun-soaked planks.

Eric dropped a towel on my head. "You were down there awfully long," he said.

I dried my face. "Got distracted by the mermaids. Lost track of time. You know how it is."

Eric laughed. "You found it, didn't you?"

I sat up and unclenched my frozen hand. "Check it out." I dangled the watch between my fingers, like a hypnotist.

Eric took the watch and felt the weight of it. "This thing's heavy." He looked at the face and examined the dials. "I think it might be broken. The time is way off."

I snatched it back, not wanting to believe it was damaged. Holding the watch next to my ears, I shook it. Inside the Rolex, I could hear the delicate purr of winding gears and gyros. The second hand began ticking. "No, it's okay," I said. "It doesn't have a battery like most watches, because this is an expensive watch." I pulled the pin out and set the time to my Sector watch.

Then I felt the Rolex's weight like Eric had, and flipped it over. Engraved on the back was, "For 45 Years On The Beat—NWE."

"Jiminy Cricket!" I passed the watch to Eric. "Read the back."

Eric read the inscription out loud. "Sooo?"

"So, this means he worked for the *North West Examiner*—the newspaper in Milner's Corner—for forty-five years. Think about it, Eric. If there *was* an incident involving a bronze statue, he would know about it. I mean, providing the incident happened in the last forty-five years."

Eric looked up at the house, and then slowly nodded. "And all we have to do is ask him."

"And hope he remembers," I added.

We both decided to remain on the dock for a while, figuring that the longer we stayed down by the lake, the harder Mr. Provost would think we were working to find his watch, and therefore, the more appreciative he would be when he got his watch back. It was kind of sneaky, but since he was having fun entertaining Rachel, we didn't feel too bad.

Ten minutes later, I took off my wetsuit and slipped on my T-shirt. "Okay," I said, standing up. "Let's go show Grandpa his watch."

CHAPTER 9

UP AT THE house, Rachel and Mr. Provost were sitting in the shade, giggling like they'd known each other forever. He actually looked mad at us for intruding on their fun. I held up the Rolex so he could see *we* weren't goofing off.

"Splendid, my boy." He took the watch and looked it over for damage. "Was it difficult to locate?"

"It took some time to find," I lied. Then, feeling guilty, I quickly added, "But it was more or less where you said it would be."

"You boys make yourselves at home." He stood up and indicated some plastic chairs scattered about the deck. "I'll pop inside and fetch my wallet."

"No, that's not necessary, Mr. Provost." I glanced at Eric, who gave me a *what-the-heck?* look.

"Are you sure?" Mr. Provost said. "Kids can always use some extra money." I guess even he thought I was nuts.

"Yeah, I'm sure." I sat in a chair. "But we'd like to ask you a few questions—if you have time, that is."

"I've got nothing *but* time." He turned and winked at Rachel, like that was a great inside joke.

Rachel smiled back politely.

"Well," I began. "I noticed, from the engraving on the back of your watch, that you worked for the newspaper for forty-five years."

"You got that right, son. For forty-five years I pounded the pavement and wrote the news. Started right out of high school."

"Do you remember the paper ever doing a story about a missing statue?" I held my breath.

"Keep talking," he said, closing his eyes. "I'm listening."

Rachel leaned forward, also listening intently.

Eric looked at me and shrugged.

"Well," I said, "do you remember something about the disappearance or theft of a life-size bronze statue? Anything like that?"

We waited.

He still had his eyes closed. *Hope he didn't fall asleep.*

Then he opened an eye and sat up straight. "Was the statue a likeness of a Cree? An Aboriginal man?"

We all nodded vigorously. "Yes!"

"Never heard of it," he said quickly.

We looked at each other, perplexed. He knew the statue was of a Cree, but he had never heard of it?

I was stunned. "But then, how did—"

"I'm pulling your leg." His cheeks tugged the corners of his mouth into a grin. He laughed uncontrollably, leaned forward, and gave Eric a good slap on the back. "You should see your faces."

We chuckled awkwardly while Mr. Provost twitched in his chair.

"Okay, so you *do* know something about the statue?" I asked. I was getting confused and looking for clarification.

"Oh, sure. I remember it well." He stood up suddenly. "Why don't we all go and take a look at the past?" He led us across his manicured lawn and back to the garage.

When we got inside, he took us to the wall of old newspapers I noticed earlier. He caressed the folded edges of the nearest stack as if it were the family bible. "What we have here is a lifetime's work. I have every issue of the *North West Examiner* since the day I started there."

"Wow," Rachel said, sounding genuinely impressed.

"That's a lot of papers, Mr. Provost!" Eric exclaimed. Even he was shocked by all the history piled up in front of us.

"You bet it is, junior. Fifty-two issues a year for forty-five years."

I could see that his collection had order to it. They weren't just heaped up like at the recycling centre. Every fifty-two editions—an entire year's worth—were bundled together with string. And each string was tagged with a label. I flipped the nearest one over: 1999.

Mr. Provost saw me. "'Eighty-nine, right?" he said confidently.

"Uhmm. No, 'ninety-nine." I showed him the tag.

"Oh? Well, whatever." He walked down the stacks and flipped tags until he found the one he was looking for. "Here it is. From twenty-six years ago. Give me a hand, boys." Our bundle was three from the bottom, so we had to move seven other packages to get it out.

"Now, let me think," he said, carefully cutting the string with a pocketknife. "The fire at the mill was in July of that year... And Mayor Lavoie retired in September... But the statue was stolen before he could make his speech... And the water treatment plant was rebuilt in..."

This sort of rambling continued for some time, and I think we all got tired and stopped listening.

"Got it," he said suddenly. "We want the first newspaper of August."

It was excruciating watching him extract papers from the bundle, delicately placing them on the ground. I finally had enough and yelled, "Get your butt in gear!" Just kidding—I didn't do that. But in my mind, I was sure thinking something like that.

"Ahhh, here it is," he finally announced, "Friday, August 5."

He unfolded the paper and smoothed the cover with his palm. The banner headline screamed at us from the garage floor, "STATUE STOLEN IN BRAZEN HEIST."

This is what I read:

The bronze statue of Cree pioneer Simon Ghost-Keeper was stolen on Wednesday night from the Canadian National Rail compound in Pine Falls. Security video footage, taken by a surveillance camera, revealed a masked intruder boldly driving a forklift up to the crate containing the statue. The thief then picked up the box and disappeared out of the camera's sight. A railroad employee suffered a concussion when he stumbled upon the bandit in the switching yard. The culprit violently struck the worker on the head with a wooden object, sending him to the Pinawa Health Complex. The statue was to have been delivered to the local branch of the Manitoba Council of Cree (MCC). The MCC was scheduled to take possession of the bronze on Saturday and to set the figure in place on Sunday.

Cree elder Johnny Barker is at a loss to explain the theft. "Who would do such a thing?" he said in an interview. "We have been raising money for seven years to pay tribute to a revered historical figure. Now we have nothing."

An MCC spokesperson said it is unlikely that another statue would be purchased if this one were not recovered.

Constable Benjamin Forbes of the RCMP is asking for the public's assistance in solving this crime.

"And then what happened?" Rachel asked, having finished reading the story first.

"Not a thing," Mr. Provost said. "No one ever came forward with information. And the police had no solid leads to go on. So, that was the end of it."

"Did you find out why it was stolen?" I asked, still staring at the headline. "I mean, did anyone ever get a ransom note or anything like that?"

"No, and that's what really bothered the community—the fact that someone would just steal it for no reason other than to prevent the Cree people from honouring one of their own."

We sat in silence on the cool concrete floor of the garage, each in our own thoughts.

"Maybe it'll still turn up," Rachel said, trying to cheer up her new friend. "Maybe someone will find it."

"I suppose that would be nice," he said, "but I'm not holding my breath."

"We're divers, Mr. Provost," I said, getting up from the floor. "We can hold our breath for a long time." I thought that was pretty clever, but as soon as I looked at Mr. Provost's face, I regretted saying it.

"You kids listen to me, and listen carefully." He stared at each of us for two seconds, and then continued. "If you know anything about this statue, anything at all, you'd better come clean and tell the police. I've covered many crime stories, but none like this. This theft was odd— really odd."

"Why's that?" Eric asked.

"Well, there were no clues at all. The statue just vanished. Usually, when an item that big is stolen, it eventually shows up. Often the bad guys get caught when they try and sell the goods they stole. We always expected a scrap metal dealer to tip off the police. But nothing like that ever happened. And it was never seen again."

We were all quiet for a minute, but I wanted him to know we were paying attention, so I said, "That's interesting."

"And there's something else you should know," Mr. Provost continued. "The young man who was hospitalized— well, he died three days later from his injuries."

Rachel groaned. "Does that make it murder?"

He refolded the paper. "Maybe not murder, but certainly manslaughter."

"Manslaughter," Rachel repeated the word slowly—with disgust. It actually sounded worse than murder.

Rachel and Eric stood up.

"You'd think *someone* would have seen *something*," Eric said to no one in particular. "In small towns, people always talk and gossip."

"Oh, sure," Mr. Provost said. "There were lots of crazy theories about who did it. Most folks thought the Filthy Few were somehow involved."

"The Filthy Few?" Eric laughed. "Is that a motorcycle gang or something?"

"More of a club, really." Mr. Provost chuckled and began searching through the papers he had on the floor. "A real bunch of characters."

"Do you think they—the Filthy Few—did it?" Rachel asked.

He shrugged. "I always thought they were nice guys, just messing around. But who knows."

"That's an odd name for a club," I said.

Mr. Provost kept rummaging through the newspapers. "They did some wacky things back then. For example, they'd all cruise around in an old van, and then they'd jump out suddenly at intersections with pails of water and squeegees and attack cars, quickly cleaning all the windows. Then they'd pile into the vehicle again and take off."

Rachel shook her head. "But that seems harmless."

Not seeming to hear her, he went on. "And another time, they raised a bunch of money for the food bank in Lockport. They set up a car wash in the grocery store parking lot, put on bikinis, and charged two bucks to wash your car."

"Then why would anyone suspect the Filthy Few?" Eric asked. "They sound like a bunch of do-gooders."

"I think they were," Mr. Provost said. "But it bothered most folks that those boys always wore rubber masks—dirty old bum masks, if I recall. That made people suspicious and nervous. Some even thought their good deeds were just a cover for criminal activities. Ahh, found it!"

We waited for him to show us whatever he'd been looking for.

"I took this picture of the Filthy Few a month before the statue heist."

I let Eric and Rachel study the old photograph first.

"It can't be!" Rachel mumbled.

"Whoa!" Eric gasped.

They both stepped back and waited for me to see the image.

I got on my knees again. It was a group picture. Five guys—two still wearing the rubber hobo masks, three with their masks peeled up and exposing their grinning faces. I didn't know who the first boy was, but the second kid was Scolletti, and the third teenager was my dad.

I thought I was going to faint.

"That picture doesn't mean anything," Rachel said.

"Yeah," Eric agreed. "It just means your dad *knew* Scolletti a long time ago. Like when they were teenagers."

"I know," I mumbled.

We had left Mr. Provost's cottage and were now sitting around a picnic table at the tiny beach at the north end of Clearwater Lake. I appreciated their support. But the fact was my dad might have been involved in the theft of that statue. And he may have killed someone.

"That explains why my dad always wants to know *where* we're snorkelling," I said. "So he can stop me if I tell him I'm diving in Smoke Lake. What a sneak!"

"You gotta chill out," Eric said.

Rachel nodded. "There's no way your dad would clobber anyone, Cody. He's a nice guy."

"Maybe taking the statue was a prank," I mumbled. "Maybe that guard startled them and things got out of hand. Stuff like that happens."

Rachel shook her head. "But it doesn't fit with the other things they did," she said, her finger tracing a heart someone had carved into the wood. "You heard Mr. Provost. They were good Samaritans, on silly missions to clean stuff and raise money for charities."

"But the picture *proves* my dad was buddies with Scolletti." I flicked an ant off the table, and then felt bad for taking my anger out on a bug. "And Scolletti didn't want us in Smoke Lake. That's a fact too."

"We should have left it down there," Eric said.

"I don't feel like swimming anymore," Rachel said. "Let's go back to town."

"Yeah, I'm not in the mood, either," I said.

We climbed back onto our bikes and headed for Sultana. When we crossed the bridge, I had an idea. I turned left on Larose Avenue and rolled to a stop.

"What's up?" Eric asked. "Why'd you stop here?"

I pointed to an old turn-of-the-century house, sitting across from the Kilmeny River—a lazy, winding river that hugged the eastern edge of our small town as it wound its way north. "That building," I said, "used to be the headquarters for the MCC."

"That's right," Rachel said. "Someone years ago donated it to the Manitoba Council of Cree."

I lowered my bike on the grass curb and indicated that my friends should follow me onto the trail in front of the building.

"So?" Eric said. "They moved their HQ to Pine Falls a long time ago. Now this is a bed and breakfast."

I waited for him to catch up. "Well, the article Mr. Provost showed us said that the MCC were ready to mount the statue just before it was stolen. Right?"

"Yeah, so?" Eric looked at the park-like yard.

"If they were going to mount it here, there must have been something on which they were going to mount it. So let's take a look. Maybe we can still set things right."

The front yard was half the size of a football field. Shrubs, hedges, and flowerbeds broke up the perfect grass surface. We headed in three directions, weaving around the landscaped features.

Five minutes later, our paths collided. "Anything?" I asked.

"I don't think so," Eric said. "But then, I don't know what I'm looking for."

"Well, if I were going to put up an expensive bronze statue..." Rachel looked around. "I'd put it near the sidewalk, or the road. Somewhere people could see it."

We walked back to our bikes and looked at the yard again. Nothing. A flowerbed here, shrubs there.

"Come on, you guys. Let's go." Eric lifted his bike. "I could use a pop."

"Hang on a second." I jogged down the sidewalk and looked back across the property one more time. It had to be here: a steel platform. A stone base. Something.

But there was nothing.

I made my way back to the road where Eric and Rachel were waiting. Behind them, a man and his Labrador retriever were just starting down the trail that twisted its way along the river and wrapped around town.

And that's when it hit me.

CHAPTER 10

"I DON'T THINK they were going to put the statue on the property," I explained to Rachel and Eric. "I think they were going to put it somewhere along the community trail. It starts right here and winds all the way around Sultana."

Rachel nodded. "And more people would see it on the trail than in that yard."

Eric lowered his bike again and reluctantly led the way down the path. "Enough chatter. Let's just find the stupid thing."

It wasn't long before we came to the first bench on the trail. Here the river widened and carved a gentle arc through the clay. I had to admit that it was a good spot for a park bench—except the bench was facing the wrong way. *Crazy planners!*

We walked around the next corner and I saw two more benches in the distance, but they were facing the river, as they should.

"Hey," I called out to Eric and Rachel. They were ten paces ahead of me. "Come back here."

"Now what?" Eric hollered.

"Look." I pointed to the bench. "If you were going to put a park bench in a spot like this, would you have it facing the river, or an ugly cluster of shrubs?"

"You're right," Rachel said, eagerly clawing her way into the dense hedge. "Ouch! My toe."

"What is it?" I asked.

"There's something here," she said. "Something hard."

Eric and I peeled back the tall branches where Rachel stood. And there it was: a concrete pillar. The pillar resembled a cement tree stump cut waist-high off the ground.

"Is that it?" Eric asked. He sounded disappointed.

"It must be." Rachel ran her hand over the top of the weathered base. "Look at these." Her fingers touched four thick steel bolts that protruded from the surface.

"Those are the mounting posts for the bronze," I said. "They go through the holes in the feet, and then get bolted down." I leaned over the shrubs and felt the nearest bolt. It was gritty with surface rust, but even after twenty-six years, the threading felt undamaged.

I let go of the branches and they snapped back, concealing the concrete post. I sat down on the bench and watched Eric and Rachel step back onto the trail. They brushed spiderwebs and leaves from their clothes and plunked themselves down next to me.

Eric watched a mosquito land on his thigh. "So now what?"

"It's all coming together, isn't it?" Rachel said. "This morning we knew nothing. And now we know almost everything. We know when it was stolen, we know how it was stolen, and we know from where it was stolen."

"And," I said, "if we look at the evidence, we also know who stole it. The Filthy Few—either all of them, some of them, or just Scolletti."

Eric smacked the mosquito with enough force to kill a bat. "Speaking of evidence, didn't that guy in the picture—the kid on the left—look kind of familiar?"

"No," I said. "Well, a bit, I suppose. We should have asked if we could make a photocopy."

"Maybe we should just tell the police," Rachel said.

I shook my head. "We can't. We don't have any proof. Everything we know is whatchamacallit—circumstantial."

She nodded slowly. "I suppose. But we could put the statue back."

"That's what I was thinking," I said.

"That seems like a lot of work, you guys," Eric said.

I looked at the area around the base of the statue. "Yeah, it'd be a tricky operation," I admitted.

"How about this," Eric said. "We phone Scolletti and tell him we have *it*. But we won't use the words 'bronze' or 'statue.' Then we tell him that he can have it back if he pays us. Pays us—oh, I don't know—a thousand dollars."

Rachel laughed, thinking he was joking.

I wasn't laughing. "That's pretty clever," I said. "Then, if he agrees to do a deal, we'll know that he knows we're talking about the statue. And if he knows that, it can only be because he's the guy who stole it and ditched it in the lake."

Eric clenched his fist. "Yeah, and then we've got him."

"I just hope he takes the bait," I said. "Otherwise, someone else is guilty. Probably my—"

"Your dad is *not* involved in this," Rachel said with finality. "So stop it. Remember, there were five guys in the Filthy Few. Any one of those other boys could have stolen the statue too."

"We'd still have to get Scolletti to admit his involvement in the crime," Eric mumbled, ignoring his sister. "Or maybe we can record him talking about the statue. Something like that, anyway. Otherwise he'll just deny everything, and we'll be nowhere. We have to do this right the first time. I don't want that nut loose once he knows we've tricked him."

"That's for sure," Rachel said. "He may already have killed one person, so who knows what he'd do to stay out of jail."

I stood up and stretched. "Okay, then. Let's make *that* Plan A—for now, anyway. And our Plan B can be returning the statue and mounting it on its base."

We walked back to our bikes and rode to the Rivercrest to buy some pop.

"Maybe Brad would help us," I said after swallowing a mouthful of root beer.

We were sitting near our bikes at the edge of the parking lot. Rachel and Eric had done their best to convince me that Scolletti had acted alone, *without* the other members of the Filthy Few. And I accepted that—well, I at least wanted to believe my dad wasn't involved.

Eric picked his drink off the curb and took a long pull. "Why do we need Jerkface?"

"Because he would make a credible witness. He's a cop. And cops have guns. If Scolletti freaks out, it'd be nice to know someone is there with a gun."

"I hate to break it to you," Eric said, "but Brad doesn't carry a gun. He's a *special* constable—remember?"

Rats! I'd forgotten that. "Yeah, but he's still a guy in a police uniform."

"Not to change the subject," Eric said, changing the subject, "but shouldn't you guys congratulate me for my keen powers of observation?"

"Remind us again what you keenly observed," I said.

"Ghost-Keeper," Eric said. "I totally called it. Our statue of Simon Ghost-Keeper is a descendent of the elder we met hundreds of years ago. Just like I—"

"Quiet!" Rachel said suddenly. "Listen!" She pointed up at the speakers mounted under the awning of the storefront. They always had the radio station set to the local country music channel, and now someone was reading the news:

> ... *these mysterious tracks lead from the water hazard to the adjacent access road and then stop. Employees reported the damage to the RCMP early this morning. Golfers are joking that the tracks are from a Loch Ness–type monster, who, fed up with the steady bombardment of golf balls, decided to leave Smoke Lake. Police, however, are treating the incident seriously and are continuing their investigation. In sports today, the...*

"So much for secrecy," Eric said. "The whole town knows now."

"No one knows anything," I said, trying to sound rational. "The only person who's going to be nervous is the person who dumped the statue. And if that's Scolletti, we want him to be nervous."

"And don't forget it was your idea to tell him that we have it," Rachel reminded her brother.

Eric squinted into his pop can, like a fortune teller staring into a crystal ball. "Yeah, I know," he said. "It was just a shock hearing it on the radio. I guess I thought we'd be able to sort this out *before* the cops got wind."

"Don't worry about the police," I said. "There's nothing in the lake for them to find. We have the statue." The door at the rear of the restaurant suddenly opened, and Creepy Calvin emerged. He glared at us for a few seconds and went back inside. *Jeepers, he is weird!*

"And the sooner we get rid of Ironman, the sooner I'll be happy," Eric said. "This whole statue thing is causing me a great deal of stress. And I *never* get stressed out."

"Unless," Rachel said, "you can't find anything to eat."

It was almost 5:00 by the time we got back to Eric and Rachel's house. And as soon as we walked into the kitchen, their phone rang. Rachel and I looked at each other anxiously. I think we both had a bad feeling it was Scolletti. The thought of talking to him again (or whoever it was) made the little hairs on my neck stand up.

"Maybe we shouldn't answer it," Rachel said, her voice quivering.

I nodded. "Yeah, maybe we should just let it ring."

Eric walked to the charger stand. "Jeepers, you guys! It could be anyone. Could be Mom."

"And if it's not Mom...?" Rachel said.

Eric reached for the phone. "Then we can get this over with."

"Remember," I said quickly, "Plan A."

He took a deep breath, flicked the phone to speaker and said, "Hello?"

"You punks think you're pretty clever." The voice sounded similar to the first caller—who might have been Scolletti—but it also sounded slightly different.

"I'm not sure what you mean," Eric said boldly.

Rachel froze—eyes as big as Frisbees.

The caller screamed, "*You filthy—*"

Eric switched the phone off.

"What're you doing?" I said. "He's gonna go ballistic!"

"Exactly," Eric said. "We might as well make him really mad. Maybe he'll slip up and do something stupid."

"Like kill us?" I mumbled, pacing the room like a lawyer.

Rachel snapped out of it and shook her head. "You watch way too much TV, Eric."

"He'll phone back," Eric said. "Don't worry."

Rachel and I looked at each other. Clearly, we were both worried—worried he'd phone back, *and* worried he might not phone back. A lose-lose situation, if ever there was one.

The phone rang again and Eric switched it on. But he didn't say anything; he just listened.

"Hello?" the caller said.

"If you want to talk to us," Eric said, "you better talk nice. No more yelling, or..."

"I'll wring your neck if you hang—"

Click. Eric hung up again.

"You got guts," Rachel said.

I shook my head and resumed pacing. "Just tell him this time. I can't handle much more."

The phone chirped for the third time, but Eric was ready.

"We have *it*," Eric said. "Do you want it back?"

There was a long pause, and the silence was torture. I cringed involuntarily.

"You have *what*?" the man asked cautiously. He seemed to have regained his composure.

"If you don't know, then I guess you don't want it. We'll just sell it to someone else. No big deal."

Another long pause.

And then the caller asked, "Where is it?"

Got him!

Eric held up his palm to high five Rachel, but Rachel scowled and pointed at the phone. Eric said to the speaker, "It's safe."

"How do I know you really have it?" the man asked.

Eric said, "Go see for yourself. It's not where you dumped it, and that's because we have it."

"How much?"

Eric grinned. "We want three thousand dollars for it."

"Who else knows about this?" he asked.

"Just us—the three of us."

"I'll get back to you," he said. And then he added, "Keep it hidden."

"This is what we're calling a limited-time offer," Eric said. "If we don't hear from you in two hours, we're selling it on eBay."

The man snorted and said, "Give me two days."

Eric agreed and hung up the phone. "It worked," he said.

"Why did you say we want three thousand dollars for the statue?" Rachel asked.

Eric shrugged. "I thought it would be nice for us each to make a thousand dollars. You know, for our troubles."

"But we're not selling it to him, you dummy!" she said.

"I know that," Eric said. "But I had to come up with an amount he would believe. And three thousand dollars splits nicely three ways."

Rachel changed the subject. "So now we know for a fact Scolletti was involved."

"To be honest," I said, "I'm not sure that was him. I mean, I still think he's involved . . . It's just that this caller didn't sound like Scolletti."

"Naw," Eric said, "that's just your imagination. It had to be him."

I shrugged.

Rachel looked at me anxiously.

"If it wasn't Scolletti . . ." Eric said.

"Don't even think it," Rachel scolded her brother.

"Huh?" Eric looked perplexed.

"Cody's dad is *not* a suspect," she said.

"What?" Eric said. "No. That's not what I was getting at."

"It's okay," I said. "When I see my dad, I'll ask him about the Filthy Few myself."

"You will?" Rachel said.

I nodded. "I have to know if he was involved."

Eric sat at the kitchen table and sighed.

"So, what now?" Rachel looked to me for guidance.

"I guess we can call the cops," I said, "and tell them everything we know. The statue has been found, they can re-open the investigation, and so on." Although, after all those years under water, I didn't think they'd find much evidence on the bronze. Plus, Rachel and I had probably polished away every last fingerprint when we cleaned the statue.

"And they can trace those phone calls," Rachel said, "and arrest whoever you just made that deal with."

I nodded, wondering again who had really called us.

CHAPTER 11

ERIC SAID, "I'LL bike over to Brad's place. If he's home, I'll bring him here."

As soon as Eric left, Rachel and I went out to the shed to check on the statue. I don't think either one of us imagined it would be gone—and it wasn't—but if someone was going to haul away our discovery, we wanted to spend as much time with it as we could now.

"Do you think the RCMP will be able to sort everything out?" I asked, peeling back the tarp that covered the face. We were kneeling on the ground again, on opposite sides of the bronze head.

Rachel said, "I'm sure they can trace those phone calls to either the golf course, or a cell phone, or someone's house. I think that'll be the key to solving everything—finding that person."

A car door slammed in the driveway.

"Must be Eric and Brad," I said. "I guess he was home."

A minute later, a shadow in the doorway of the shed caught my attention and I froze. I had a gut feeling it wasn't Eric. A glance to the door confirmed it. But it wasn't Scolletti, either. It was Creepy Calvin, the cook at the Rivercrest. And he had a gun aimed at us.

It was warm in the shed, but I was instantly chilled to the bone. Rachel turned and saw him too. We both slowly stood up.

He took two nervous steps into the shed. His eyes darted all around the space—stopping on the statue. A twisted grin slid across his face. I tried to picture his bald head with hair, and knew immediately that I had identified another member of the Filthy Few. Calvin Frippley was the first kid in the picture.

I would have held up my hands like in the movies, but he didn't ask us to. In fact, he wasn't saying anything. He just stood there like a crazed zombie.

"Who's laughing now?" Calvin finally said, breaking the silence.

I realized then that Rachel was holding my hand and squeezing the heck out of it. I think it was the gun that scared her—black, menacing, lethal. Now, obviously a lot was happening just then, and one's memory probably gets a bit muddled over time, but I do remember being happy that Rachel was holding my hand, and I remember not wanting to let go.

Anyway, back to the problem at hand—that's a pun, by the way. Calvin was kind of skinny, so the two of us might have overpowered him in a fight. But with that gun aimed at our chests, I wasn't taking any chances.

"You just couldn't stay away from the lake," Calvin continued. "You had to go down *again*."

To stall for time, I said, "Why'd you steal it in the first place?"

"Shut your face," he hissed. "For almost thirty years it sat at the bottom of Smoke Lake. The town forgot about it, and the cops forgot about it. And now you kids think you can blackmail us with it?"

He threw back his rat-like head and laughed—a fingernails-on-chalkboard kind of laugh. His bloodshot eyes seemed far off—probably on another planet.

"One of you killed a man!" Rachel shouted. "A man who did nothing to you. You just killed him."

Calvin's eyes drifted to Rachel, like she was a boring distraction. "We didn't mean to kill him—or even hurt him, to tell the truth. But after he died, what could we do?"

"You could have turned yourselves in, you ... you coward." Rachel's anger seemed to give her courage, and she let go of my hand.

Calvin flinched at that accusation. "I'm not going to jail for an *accident*. And that's all it was—an accident. He was in the wrong place at the wrong time."

120

"When you bash someone on the head and kill them," I said, getting mad too, "that's not an accident. That's murder."

"*Shut up!*" Calvin screamed.

"But why?" Rachel asked. "Why'd you steal the statue in the first place?"

Calvin's face turned purple with rage, and I thought he was going to shoot us dead right there.

"Why?" he said. "I'll tell you *why*. Because a gang isn't supposed to sneak around picking up garbage. A gang is supposed to scare people and make money, not sneak around cleaning windows at 3:00 A M—as a bloody joke!"

"The Filthy Few?" I said.

Calvin nodded. "Your old man told you about us, huh?"

"No," I said. "We saw your picture in an old newspaper."

He seemed to not hear me. "The two of us finally had enough," he said. "After the others refused to swipe that bronze with us, we did it alone."

"Mr. Lint *didn't* help you steal it?" Rachel asked, finding my hand again and giving it a comforting squeeze.

"Are you kidding?" he said, sounding disgusted. "That chicken wouldn't spit on a sidewalk."

Even though I was facing a criminal with a gun, I sighed with relief. Dad wasn't a murderer. The burden of that possibility had troubled me more than I'd known, but now, with my dad in the clear, I could focus on the last pieces of this puzzle.

So, who was the second bad guy? We always assumed and suspected it was Scolletti, but I wanted to hear it from Calvin. I was about to ask him who his partner was when he addressed us again.

"In a minute," he said, looking down at his watch, "we're all going for a ride."

Uh-oh. I didn't like the sound of that, and I knew I had to do something—anything!—fast.

Rachel let go of my hand for the second time. "We're not going with you!"

"You might not be coming back with me," he said, "but you're definitely going somewhere with me." He laughed like a hyena and looked down at his watch again.

That was my chance. I stepped up on the bronze and dove over the statue and onto Calvin. Catching him by surprise, my weight pushed him back and we crashed into the garden tools leaning against the wall. He crumpled under my weight, groaning in pain as he hit the ground. But that groan was the only good news.

The shock of my sneak attack quickly left him and he fought like a trapped animal. Twisting and writhing, he rolled me off. Furious at my feeble escape attempt, he lashed out at my head with his fist. But I wasn't giving up, either. I turned my head, deflecting most of a blow that would have otherwise knocked me out.

I shook away the stars just in time to see Rachel kick the gun across the dirt. *Way to go!*

I wriggled like mad to free myself, but he had me pinned like a wrestler. I was down for the count. *Game over, Cody.*

Rachel took another step closer and bravely swung at Calvin's head, but he must have seen her coming. He leaned back to avoid the blow and punched her shoulder with a vicious jab. She staggered and fell, giving Calvin time to focus on me again.

I watched in horror as he cocked his arm for another punch. Closing my eyes, I braced myself for the pain ...

"Enough!" someone barked.

Everyone froze.

I looked past Calvin—and his extended fist—and saw Special Constable Brad Murphy and Eric standing in the doorway. Brad snatched Calvin's gun off the ground.

We were rescued, thank goodness.

Brad scanned the room and his eyes stopped on the bronze. He shook his head slowly and said, "I never thought I'd see that thing again."

Calvin dropped his arm and rolled off me roughly. "About time you showed up," he said to Brad.

No!

Eric looked at Brad. "What's he talking about—?"

Before Eric could finish that sentence, Brad shoved Eric toward Rachel and me. "Keep quiet," Brad said.

Our situation had just gotten worse. Way, way worse. Jerkface was Calvin's accomplice—the other member of the Filthy Few—not Scolletti.

Brad pointed the gun at us and ordered us into the corner. He seemed a lot calmer than Calvin, and for some reason, that made him seem scarier.

"My leg is messed up real bad, Brad," Calvin whined. He hobbled to a lawn chair and sat down.

For the first time, I noticed blood all over Calvin's calf. I followed the trail of red across the shed, realizing what must have happened. When we fell across the tools and they rattled to the ground, he had landed on the tines of a rake. And those rusty—but still sharp—spikes must have pierced his leg.

Brad kept the gun trained on us but snuck quick glances at the bronze. "Some things really are better left hidden... and forgotten," he said softly. "Now you three troublemakers are going to have deal with the consequences of your meddling."

Calvin tried again to get his partner's attention. "I gotta go to a doctor, man. I need stitches... or antibiotics... or something."

"If you go to a doctor now," Brad said, "we're *both* going to jail. And I don't want to go to jail. So wrap up your leg, take an aspirin, and shut up."

Calvin looked around the room, then said, "You got a first aid kit?"

"Yeah," Eric said, "we do. Thanks for asking."

It took Calvin a few seconds to realize that Eric was being a smarty-pants, but when he finally did figure it out, he looked furious. He stood up, grabbed a screwdriver from a toolbox and limped toward us. He held the screwdriver in his fist like he was going to stab someone. "Do you… or do you not… have a first aid kit?"

"There's an old one," Rachel said quickly. "On that shelf." She pointed at a plastic container with a faded red cross on it.

Calvin snorted, turned around, and dragged himself over to the shelf.

Five minutes went by while we all waited for him to wrap his leg in yellowing gauze and grey-looking surgical dressing. With Brad aiming a gun at us, there was nothing we could do. After all, we'd planned on being rescued by him, not held at gunpoint.

"What do you guys want?" I finally said. "You can have the statue back. We won't tell anyone about it."

"Too late for that now," Brad said.

"It's not too late," Rachel said. "Only the three of us know about the statue, and we won't tell anyone. We promise."

Brad looked at Rachel. "We have to put our bronze friend back in the lake."

"That's fine with us," Eric said. "We don't know what to do with him, anyway."

"But before we put *him* back where he belongs," Calvin said, "we have to put *you* three where you belong."

CHAPTER 12

"WHAT'S THAT SUPPOSED to mean?" Eric asked.

Calvin laughed.

"Now why did you have to go and say that, Calvin?" Brad said. "You're going to upset them. Don't listen to him. We're just going to go for a ride until we can figure out a way to sort all this out."

"But there's nothing to sort out," I said. "We'll give you the statue right now. Take it."

"We'll even help you load it in your car," Eric added. "And we'll forget about the money. You can have it for free."

Brad snorted, looking like he was about to smack Eric.

"Come on," Eric added, "we're family."

"How? Because twenty years ago, I married your aunt? That was punishment enough. There's no reason why I should spend the rest of my life in jail too."

Calvin laughed as though that was the funniest thing he'd ever heard.

Brad ordered Calvin outside to make sure no one was around. A minute later, he limped back. "The coast is clear," he said to Brad.

"Okay," Brad said. "This is what's going to happen. First, you're going to help put the statue in the back of Calvin's truck. Then you three are going to climb into the trunk of the Crown Vic—my police car."

"And then what?" I asked.

Brad ignored me.

"And then what?" Rachel repeated.

Brad ignored Rachel.

Calvin went out again and backed his rusty truck up to the shed. We disrespectfully dragged the bronze into the cargo box. The gun in Brad's hand tracked our every move, so there was no chance for an escape or another attack.

After Calvin slammed the tailgate shut, Brad said, "Drive ahead to your place and make sure the boathouse is secure. I'll be right behind you. We'll lock them up by the river until... until we think of something. I'll have to go to work again, but I'll come back as soon as I can."

Calvin nodded, shuffled back into the cab, and drove off.

Brad made Rachel fasten plastic handcuffs on Eric and me. Then he did the same to Rachel. He popped the trunk on his cruiser and ordered us into the cavernous rear.

I wasn't a fan of confined spaces, but I knew there was no point in arguing with him. When we were all in the trunk, he slammed the lid. Next, we heard him close the shed door, then felt the car sink as he got in behind the wheel. The engine started, and we began to move.

"This is bad," I heard Eric whisper in the dark. "Real bad."

I wriggled and adjusted my body on the rough carpet that lined the trunk. I was the last one shoved in, and I was now closest to the back bumper. Some light spilled in around the tail light enclosures, but it wasn't enough to see anything.

"I still can't believe Brad is part of this," Rachel said. She was next to me.

"Another member of the Filthy Few," I said.

"We were right about him all along," Eric said. "He's a certified grade-A jerkface."

"The phone calls," I said. "They were from Creepy Calvin and Brad Murphy."

"But how could they know...?" Eric's voice trailed off.

"They must have seen the golf balls in the wagon," I said. "And then when they heard about the tracks in the grass—from our second dive—they knew we'd gone back."

"That means," Eric said, "when Scolletti told us we couldn't dive in Smoke Lake, he was really just doing his job. He didn't want us in the lake because it was trespassing, or because it was unsafe, or whatever."

Brad hit the pothole at the end of the street, and we all took a hard bounce.

Eric grunted when his head bashed into something metal.

"You okay?" Rachel asked.

"Yeah, there's some stuff here..." Eric shuffled around deep in the trunk. "There's one of those spiny spike belts for stopping cars. And there's a toolbox or... or something next to my head."

"A toolbox?" I said. "See if you can open it and—"

Eric cut me off. "I'm already on it. It's tricky with these stupid straps on my wrist... But I think I can..."

I heard one clasp snap open, then another.

"Got it?" Rachel asked.

"Yup," he said. "Eric to the rescue again."

"Just like when you brought home another bad guy," I said, "and he locked us up in this trunk."

Eric laughed. "Well, okay, except for that time."

Rachel and I listened as Eric poked around inside the box.

"It just feels like police stuff," he said. "Some sort of tape... file folders, paper stuff. Plastic bags and marker pens."

"An evidence kit," I said, guessing at the box's purpose.

"Can you feel anything sharp?" Rachel asked. "A pocket knife? A utility knife? A saw?"

"I wish," Eric said. "But there's nothing like that."

"Let's feel around in the rest of the trunk," I said. "Maybe there's a real toolbox in here somewhere."

We groped around near our heads, but no one announced a discovery.

"You guys stay where you are," Rachel said. "I'm going to see if I can spin around. If I can, I'll search the other end—by our feet."

Rachel seemed to be pretty flexible, because she didn't have too much trouble turning around in the trunk. I couldn't tell what she was doing, because the noise from the rear wheels suddenly got a lot louder.

"I think he's on a gravel road now," Eric yelled.

"I'm pretty sure Calvin's house is on the Kilmeny River," I said. "About ten minutes south of town. Brad must be on the river road."

"We don't have much time," Eric said.

Rachel shouted excitedly, "I found something else. Maybe a road flare."

"Describe it," Eric ordered.

"Like a stick of dynamite," Rachel said, "or fireworks."

"That does sound like a safety flare," I said. "Anything else?"

"I think... I think there's something else shoved in the corner." Rachel's legs twisted and twitched next to my head as she strained to reach the item. "Got it!"

Eric and I waited for her report.

"It's just an old package of cigarettes... Feels empty," she said. "But there's..."

The car slowed down and took a turn.

"Quick, Rachel!" I said. "Turn around again." When Brad had shoved us into the trunk, all our heads were on the right side. I didn't want him to think we were up to something when he popped the trunk.

Rachel settled in beside me. "There was a lighter..." she panted in my ear. "There was a cigarette lighter in the package. I'm not sure if it'll still work, but I took it."

The car rolled to a stop and we felt Brad get out. The heat in the trunk had become unbearable, and I was anxious for fresh air. But nothing happened.

"God, it's hot in here," Eric whispered.

"What's he waiting for?" I mumbled.

"Maybe this was his plan all along," Rachel said. "To have us suffocate in the trunk and then dump our bodies in a lake."

Another minute passed.

"We gotta get outta here," Eric said. "I'm about to black out."

"Hey," Rachel wheezed. "I thought... car trunks were supposed to have safety buttons. To escape if..."

"You're right." I immediately twisted and felt the area around the back end of the car. I was hoping for a glow-in-the-dark button, but of course there was nothing like that. But I did feel a length of cable near where the latch was. I yanked on it in frustration and heard the satisfying click of the lock mechanism releasing.

The hood slowly opened a few centimetres, and then the power of the springs quickly forced it all the way up.

We could breathe again.

I lifted my head, looking for an escape route. But instead of an easy getaway, I saw Calvin and Brad. They were three metres from the car. And they were both staring at me.

Brad walked over to the open hatch. "Since 2002," he said, "all trunks have been required to have an emergency trunk release. In case of . . . situations like this, I suppose."

We squinted at our captors, trying to get used to the sunlight again.

Brad continued, "I was just saying to Calvin that if you three were too dumb to escape from the trunk, maybe you deserved to cook in there. In fact, I thought you were already toast."

"Wishful thinking," Calvin mumbled, looking down at his bandaged leg.

"Now, now," Brad said, pretending to scold Calvin. "They were under a lot of stress in there. But in the end, they did get out."

Calvin tucked his pistol in his pants and waved us out of the trunk with a rifle.

We were all soaked with sweat, and the fresh air felt pretty good.

"Lock them up," Brad said. "We'll figure out the rest when my shift is done."

Brad slammed the trunk, slid behind the wheel, and sped off down the gravel driveway. Now it was just us and Creepy Calvin.

I looked around. We were where I expected to be—on land adjacent to the Kilmeny River. But unlike all the small residential lots closer to town, this was a large rural property, far from any other homes or summer cabins. The house behind Calvin reminded me of him—decrepit and ugly.

"Welcome to my humble abode," Calvin said.

Eric looked at the surrounding forest and the yard choking with weeds. "If you want," Eric said, "I'll cut the grass for you. Looks like it hasn't been trimmed in three or four *years*."

"You got a smart mouth, kid," Calvin sneered. "We'll see how feisty you are after dark."

"Look, Calvin," Rachel said, trying to sound calm and logical. "Brad's gone now. If you let us go, we'll tell the cops you helped us."

I nodded. "Yeah. We'll say Brad made you kidnap us, and you'll be a hero for letting us go again."

"And don't you want to get your leg checked out?" Eric pointed at Calvin's calf. "If you ignore that kind of wound, you could get tetanus, or trench foot, or scurvy."

"Nice try," Calvin said. "Now follow the trail around to the river."

He marched us past the house and instructed us to head east, down toward the river. I saw flashes of blue through the pine trees as we neared the water. I figured they were going to try and kill us, but as long as Brad was gone, we had a chance of escaping. We just had to act fast.

Down by the river, Calvin ordered us onto a short wooden walkway that served as a bridge to his battered boathouse. As we shuffled over the planking, I noticed plastic jugs of gasoline and other odds and ends spread out on the shore. Calvin had removed anything we could use to escape from the structure.

"Get in the boathouse and keep quiet," he said. "And don't even think about trying to swim away. I'll be sitting outside watching, and I'll blast you out of the water before you make it anywhere."

I followed Eric and Rachel into the old building. We listened as Calvin snapped a padlock on the door.

"We have to get out of here," Eric whispered.

Rachel nodded. "When Brad comes back, we're all dead."

I looked around the boathouse, which, by the way, held no boat. It was dark inside, but there was enough light reflecting from under the sliding boat door that we could see pretty much everything. Only there wasn't much to see. A metre-wide walkway ran along three walls of the building. And the space for the boat was about the size of a parking stall. Water gurgled and splashed against the timbers under our feet.

Eric began rubbing his plastic handcuffs against the edge of a rough wall beam. "Step one," Eric said, "is getting rid of these stupid things."

Rachel fumbled in the front pocket of her shorts and pulled out the lighter she had found in the trunk. "Maybe this will help."

Eric and I watched as she spun the flint. Nothing.

"Rats!" Eric said.

Rachel tried the lighter again and again. "Too bad," she said. "I was really hoping to use the lighter to light the flare."

"The flare?" I said.

"Yeah, I took it from the car too," she said. "I shoved it in my shorts under my T-shirt." She lifted her shirt and pulled out the stick."

I looked at Eric, and we both grinned.

Rachel glanced up at me. "What?"

"You don't need a match or a lighter to light a safety flare," I said softly. "You just rub it against a rough surface—like brick or pavement—and it ignites."

"You did good, Rachel," Eric said. He grabbed the flare from her and peeled off the paper seal. He dropped to his knees and ran the flare along a plank like he was lighting a giant match. The flare sparked and crackled, then burst into a bright flame.

"Beautiful," Eric said.

I stretched my wrists as far apart as I could and let Eric burn the thick plastic cuffs. As the restraints began to melt, I felt a new hope that we would at least be free inside the boathouse. The cuffs were just starting to drip liquid plastic onto the decking, when suddenly, the flame died.

I quickly forced my hands apart before the material could harden again. The plastic linking my wrists together stretched like pizza cheese, then finally separated. My hands were free.

"Come on," Eric shook the flare and quietly cursed it.

"What happened?" Rachel said. "Shouldn't it burn for longer than that?"

"Yeah," I said. "It must be a dud, or really old, or something." I took the flare from Eric and tried to press the tip against his cuffs, hoping there might still be some heat left.

"It's no good," Eric said after half a minute. "It's gone cold."

I dropped the flare and began searching the boathouse again. "There must be something in here we can use to free your wrists," I said. I patrolled the walkway and examined every inch of the building, but found nothing—no forgotten tools, no hidden saws, no hatchets.

Meanwhile, Eric continued to rub his cuffs on every surface that felt abrasive, but nothing seemed to affect the tough polymer material. "These things are strong," Eric said, exasperated. "We need a sharp knife or some kind of snippers."

I stared at the water in the boathouse.

"Maybe we could trick Calvin," Rachel said, "like on TV. I could say I have to pee. And then we could jump him and overpower him."

"Maybe," I said, still staring at the dark water, thinking hard.

Eric walked over and stood beside me. Now he was studying the water too. "You could do it," he said.

"What?" Rachel said.

Eric ignored his sister. "It's a long swim, for sure," he said. "But you could totally do it."

"What?" Rachel demanded. "Tell me what you're talking about."

Eric explained, "It's simple. If Cody can swim out of the boathouse, he can get help."

"Are you nuts?" Rachel said. She tried to whisper, but it came out pretty loud. "Calvin will shoot him as soon as his head pops up on the other side."

Eric held up his cuffed palms, trying to calm Rachel down. "No. Cody can hold his breath longer than anyone. All he has to do is stay down deep. Calvin will never know."

Rachel didn't look convinced.

"I have to try and do something," I said. "We're dead if we stay here."

"But what about my plan?" Rachel said. "Can't we just trick him?"

"He has guns, Rachel," Eric said. "And he watches TV too. I doubt he'll fall for a lame trick like that. Anything we do or say to lure him in here will make him suspicious ... and trigger-happy."

"Don't worry," I said to Rachel. "This boathouse is in a little bay. All I have to do is swim underwater until I'm around the bend."

"And then what?" she asked. "There's no one around for kilometres. Where will you go for help?"

I hadn't thought that part through all the way, so I didn't know what to say.

"Look, Rachel," Eric said, "the main thing is that one of us gets out of this boathouse. Cody is the only one with free hands, and the only one who can possibly escape. Once he's away from here, he can improvise."

"What's that supposed to mean?" Rachel asked.

I wondered the same thing, so I waited for Eric to explain.

"It means," Eric said, "that Cody can adjust his rescue plan depending on what he sees outside the boathouse."

Rachel nodded and seemed to accept that vague answer, but I was hoping for something a bit more specific. Because to be honest, I wasn't sure exactly what to do once I was free, either.

CHAPTER 13

"PLEASE BE CAREFUL," Rachel whispered.

I nodded.

"Never mind 'careful,'" Eric said. "Just hurry. You have to get us out of here before Brad gets back."

I kicked off my shoes and slipped into the water at the rear of the boathouse. The water was only up to my chest, but I knew it would be deeper near the sliding boat door. But that was good; I didn't want Calvin to see any ripples on the surface from me swimming for freedom on the bottom.

I dipped my head under and tried to get used to the water temperature. It was comfortably warm for a swim, but the stress of the situation made me tense and nervous. And that wasn't good. I needed to be relaxed in order to maximize the length of time I could hold my breath and stay under.

Be cool. Be calm.

I silently swam to the boathouse opening. I peeked through the three-inch gap under the door and looked outside. The shore that curved to the right seemed a shorter dive, so I decided to go that way. If I could stay out of sight and underwater for thirty metres, I should be okay. At the swimming pool, I could dive two lengths underwater—no problem. Thing is, those were ideal conditions. This was a murky river and a life-or-death situation—in other words, less-than-ideal conditions.

I began the process of hyperventilating, preparing for the most important freedive of my life. When I was ready, I gave a final nod to Rachel and Eric and dove to the bottom of the boathouse. I swam out into the bay and slowly turned to the right.

And that was when I swam into weeds. Lots and lots of weeds. Now, weeds creep out most swimmers—including me—but today they were downright dangerous. They slowed me down, tugging on my arms and legs. *Not good.* The weeds were really going to reduce the distance I could cover with one breath of air. I took a chance and swam up and out of the weeds, looking to the surface at the same time.

I still had about a metre of water above me, and I hoped that was enough to avoid being spotted by Calvin. My lungs began to tighten as they craved new air, but I swam on and on. I curved more to the right, still skimming above the giant weed-bed.

When I thought I was about to black out, I gave another ten kicks and headed for shore. But I knew I couldn't just pop out of the water gasping for breath. I had to be cautious and stealthy like a ... like a Navy SEAL. So when my knees bumped into the mud, I stopped.

Raising my head slowly, I surfaced. I blinked the water from eyes and studied the shore: all clear. I lifted my nose and mouth above the water and exhaled. When I felt like my brain and my lungs had recovered again, I crawled onto the shore and hid in the brush that lined the river. I rested for another minute, wondering what to do next. Sure, I had escaped, but now I had to figure out how to free my friends.

If I had lots of time, I could have jogged back to town and found help. But time wasn't on my side. Brad could return before I ever reached a telephone. And then Rachel and Eric would be dead. I had to figure out something else ... and fast.

I cautiously zigzagged through the trees back toward the house. When I reached the overgrown yard, I stopped and looked around. To the left, I saw Calvin's truck. And way over to the right, I saw the boathouse in the distance. But there was no sign of Calvin.

Is he in the house? Or is he guarding the boathouse down by the water?

I prowled along the tree line, heading for the truck. When I got as close as I could by hiding among the trees,

I sprinted across the weedy gravel and ducked behind the tailgate. I glanced in the box of the truck to see if our statue was still there. It was. I crept to the passenger door and stuck my head in the open window. I was hoping to find another gun or some kind of weapon—but of course, that was wishful thinking. Except for all the junk food wrappers and empty drink containers littering the floor, the cab was empty.

But the keys were still in the ignition. Calvin had either forgotten them in the truck, or he'd never removed them, thinking his property was immune to theft. I opened the door slowly and yanked the keys from the steering wheel. As I began to close the door again, I heard a faint beep coming from somewhere in the cab.

I stopped, opened the door wide, and re-examined the truck. On the seat, under a potato chip bag, was Calvin's cell phone. It was the same model my dad had, a Samsung. I looked at the screen: one missed call, it said. I pocketed the phone, gently closed the door, and sprinted back into the trees.

I dialled 911 and asked to be connected to the Pine Falls Police Station. As soon as the dispatcher answered the phone, I asked to speak to a police officer.

"One moment please," she said. "I'll transfer your call."

Ten seconds later a voice barked, "I told you never to call this cell phone. What's going on?"

I froze. It was Brad Murphy, a.k.a. Jerkface.

"Is there a problem?" he said slowly regaining his cool.

I disconnected the call without saying a word. *Not good!*

The dispatcher must have transferred my call directly to Brad. And Brad obviously had call display and thought Calvin was phoning him.

I stared at the flashing LOW BATTERY icon, wondering how much juice was left to call Dad... or *somebody*. The phone in my hand suddenly vibrated. It was so unexpected that I dropped it. I scooped it up and scanned the display. The caller ID was blocked, so I couldn't tell who was phoning Calvin's phone, but it had to be Brad calling back. Only I couldn't answer it. He'd recognize my voice, and he'd know we'd escaped. But by not taking the call, Brad would also know *something* wasn't right. In fact, he might even be turning his car around and racing back out here right now. Bottom line, I had just made things a lot worse by trying to call the cops, and my friends were in more of a pickle now than before I escaped.

Way to go, Cody!

I quickly dialled home and waited, anxious to hear Mom's voice. But after two rings, the phone went silent and I heard nothing at all. I glanced at the Samsung. The screen was blank. No power. The phone was useless, but I wedged it in my wet pants anyway.

I ran through the forest and looped around to the boat-house. When I neared the river, I stopped and searched for Calvin. I found him sitting on a folding lawn chair. He was sipping on a beer can with the rifle across his lap.

A bell began ringing at the house.

Now what?

The ringing stopped for a second, and then began again. On and off, on and off. Finally, I understood. The telephone in the house was connected to a bell outside, so it could be heard from anywhere in the yard.

Calvin ignored the ringing and groped around in his pockets for his cell phone. He seemed to be wondering if it was worth getting up and fetching his phone from the truck.

Go, you lazy poop-sack!

The bell at the house began ringing again, suggesting that whoever was calling *really* wanted to get a hold of Calvin. Finally, he stood up. His injured leg must have been causing him a lot of pain—too bad—because it took him a long time to hobble up to the house and out of sight.

When he was gone, I raced to the boathouse, snatched a paddle from the ground and wedged it under the heavy latch.

I tapped on the door. "Hey, you guys," I whispered. "It's me. I'm going to try and pry the lock off the door."

"Hurry!" Eric called back.

"Please don't get caught," Rachel said.

The paddle was old and snapped like a rotten branch. I threw the pieces into the weeds.

"Okay, forget the door," I said. "Jump in the water and swim to the right. I'll help you out."

I knew they would have a hard time swimming with their hands bound, but I couldn't waste any more time working on the reinforced latch. Seconds later, Rachel emerged from the water and kicked her way to shore. I grabbed her hand and hauled her up. Eric surfaced next, sputtering and coughing water. I yanked on the plastic handcuffs between his wrists and dragged him out. He had my runners wedged in his shorts, and he handed them to me.

"Thanks," I said, quickly slipping them on.

"Where's Creepy Calvin?" Eric gasped.

"At the house," I said. "He'll be back soon."

I looked again at the stuff Calvin had removed from the boathouse—gas cans, fishing nets... There! Under his lawn chair was a small toolbox. I flipped the clasps, opened it, and grabbed a utility knife. I closed the box and slid it under the seat again.

"Okay," I said. "Let's get out of here."

CHAPTER 14

I RAN BACK into the woods, guiding my friends away from the farm. When we were a safe distance, I stopped and cut their hands free.

"Thanks," Rachel said, rubbing her wrists. "You did it."

"I love it when a plan works," Eric agreed.

I told them what I'd done and what I'd seen.

"That's not good," Eric said. "If you accidentally called Brad with Creepy Calvin's cell phone and didn't say anything when Brad answered, he might think something's wrong out here."

"I've got even more bad news," I said.

"That seems to be the only kind of news we ever get," Eric said.

"What is it?" Rachel asked.

"Well," I said, "the phone at the house started ringing like crazy right after I called the police station."

"Brad," Eric said.

"Calling back," Rachel added.

I nodded. "I think that Calvin went up to the house to answer the phone. And if that was Brad, they might figure things out pretty quick."

"Unless," Rachel said, "Calvin can convince Brad everything is okay and we're still locked up in the boathouse."

Eric frowned. "If I was Calvin, I'd look in on us as soon as I got off the phone."

"I'm sorry, guys," I said, "I sure never thought Brad would get the call when I phoned the cops for help."

"It's not your fault," Rachel said. "We would have done the same thing. Plus, you did get us out of there."

"Brad must be covering for all the real cops," Eric said, "while they're out on patrol or on holidays." He peeled off his T-shirt, wrung out the water, and slipped it on again.

"With the cell phone dead," Rachel said, "I guess we're on our own."

I nodded. "We have to get away from this place fast. I'm still worried Brad is on his way back here."

"We could hike north along the river," Eric suggested. "Maybe flag down a passing boat."

"I haven't heard a boat motor since we got here," I said. "We could be waiting a long time to catch a ride."

Rachel squeezed water from her ponytail. "Isn't the old Boy Scout camp around here?" she said. "What if we made it there? Maybe we could call for help from the camp."

"Yeah, it is in the direction of town," Eric said, "but it's also across the river. And the river is pretty wide down here. I wouldn't want to swim it."

That was when I remembered Calvin's truck keys. I pulled them from my pocket and dangled them in the air. "Or," I said, "we could just swipe Calvin's truck and drive ourselves back to town."

Eric grinned. "Sometimes the simple plans are the best plans."

Rachel held out her hand. "But I'm driving," she said. "You guys make me nervous."

"So," Eric whispered, "now what?"

We were hunkered down in the forest at the edge of Calvin's yard. The truck was about thirty metres away, and the house another thirty metres beyond that. There was no sign of Creepy Calvin. He was either in the house, down by the river again, or searching for us in the woods.

"I don't like that we don't know where he is," I said.

Rachel was anxious too. "It could be a trap," she said softly. "By now he must know that his keys and his cell phone are missing. Misplacing one item is believable, but there's no way he'd think he lost both."

We studied the property for several more minutes. Everything seemed quiet and normal. The birds chirped peacefully in the trees, and there was no sign of a trap or anything sinister.

"If I was Creepy," Eric said, "I would hide in the truck and wait for us to come to him. With his messed-up leg, he's not going to want to chase after us."

"I could sneak over and peek in the window," I said. "It's open."

"He has guns," Rachel reminded me. "If he's waiting in the truck, he'll shoot you the next time he sees you."

"What we need is a distraction . . . a diversion," Eric said. "Something to lure him out of the house, or out of the truck—if that's where he's hiding."

"If we can get him down to the boathouse," I said, "we'd have plenty of time to start the truck and drive away." We weren't legally allowed to drive a car or a truck, of course, but this was an emergency. The last thing on my mind was worrying that Rachel didn't have a licence.

"I can't handle this waiting," Eric said. "I'm going to sneak back down to the boathouse. When I'm there, I'll scream and make a ton of noise. Hopefully, that will get him to come down to the water."

"And then what?" Rachel whispered. "He'll capture you again."

"No, he won't," Eric said. "He can barely walk. As soon as I see him, I'll sprint along the edge of the forest and come back to the truck. Then we're outta here."

Eric was about to leave when Rachel grabbed his forearm. "Shh!" she said urgently. "Listen!"

A vehicle was approaching the farm. I'm sure we all hoped it was a telephone company van, or a conservation officer in a truck, or someone who could give us a ride to Sultana. But I knew that was wishful thinking. And sure enough, a minute later, Brad pulled into the yard in his police cruiser.

He turned off the car, got out and locked it, and then checked to make sure all the doors were secure. He jogged to the back door of the house, ripped it open, and called for Calvin. Calvin must have responded, because Brad slammed the door and waited outside. He scanned the yard and we automatically dropped our heads lower when he turned in our direction.

"You think he can see us?" Rachel whispered.

"No way," I said. "These shrubs are thick."

"Look!" Eric said, peeking up again. "It's Calvin."

I poked my head around a tree. Calvin walked outside with a half-eaten sandwich in his hand.

Brad asked him something, and Calvin shook his head. Calvin then said something to Brad—probably, "Why are you here?" Brad asked him a bunch of other things, which caused Calvin to point at his truck and then in the direction of the boathouse. Brad headed toward the river with a confused-looking Calvin hobbling after him.

"This is our chance," I said. "Get ready to run for the truck."

When we thought they were near the boathouse, we popped out of the trees and bolted for the vehicle.

Eric and I dove in the passenger door, and Rachel ran around the hood and jumped in behind the wheel. Unlike what you see in the movies, the truck actually started immediately—no complications, no dead battery, no weird noises from the engine. Rachel pressed the brake pedal, yanked the gearshift down into drive and hit the gas. The tires dug into the gravel and sprayed rocks in a semicircle around the yard.

"Easy!" Eric yelled.

Rachel lifted her foot off the accelerator and straightened the steering wheel. Aiming down the driveway, she touched the gas again—lightly this time—and we left the yard.

"Good job, Rach," I said.

"Just keep doing what you're doing," Eric added. "And don't hit the ditch."

I pulled the dead cell phone from my pants and said, "Let's see if we can find a charger for this."

After a minute of searching, Eric found the adapter in the glove box. He plugged it into the cigarette lighter and connected it to the phone. "Yesss," he hissed, "it's charging up!"

The truck was old and seemed to drift all over the road, so Rachel kept both hands clamped on the wheel. After rumbling down the gravel for five minutes, I glanced at the speedometer: seventy kilometres an hour.

"Stop!" Eric screamed suddenly.

Startled, Rachel stomped on the brake pedal with both feet. "What...?" she yelled. "What's wrong?" The tires locked up and the truck side-slipped to a stop.

Eric pointed down the road. "Spike belt," he said.

I looked at the gravel ahead of the truck. In the distance, something was stretched across the road. Rachel touched the gas and we rolled closer. She stopped again when the tire-piercing belt was right in front of us.

"Gosh, he's nasty," Rachel said.

Eric nodded. "Brad laid down the spike belt from the trunk of his car... in case we tried to escape in Creepy's truck."

"Which we did," I said, studying the puncturing trap.

I jumped out and dragged the spike belt toward the truck. "I got an idea!" I shouted. I threw the belt in the back with the statue and jumped in the cab again. "Go!"

Rachel looked in the rear-view mirror. "They're coming," she said.

I twisted and looked out the back window. Far behind us, a plume of dust was beginning to grow. "They'll be on us in a few minutes!" I yelled.

Rachel pressed the gas pedal and we shot forward again.

I had to put my first idea on hold, because I suddenly got a second idea. I waited for Rachel to drive around a sharp bend, and then I asked her to stop again.

"What's up?" she asked.

I quickly explained my first idea. "If we put the spike belt here, they might not see it in time. And we might be able to hoist them by their own petard."

"Huh?" Eric said. "What does that mean?"

"I'm not sure," I admitted, "but I think it might apply to this situation."

"Do it, Cody!" Rachel said. "And hurry!"

Eric and I jumped out and arranged the aluminum track across the road behind us. Fifteen seconds later, we were in the cab again, accelerating down the road toward Sultana.

"That's only going to help us if they don't see it," Eric said.

I nodded, and then quickly moved on to my second idea. "Let's call Mr. Provost," I said to Eric, "and put him on speaker so we can all hear him and talk to him."

"You think he can help us?" Rachel asked, not taking her eyes off the gravel road.

"He's our best bet," I said. "I just hope he believes us."

CHAPTER 15

"HELLO?"

"Hi." I spoke loudly so the mic in the phone could pick me up. "This is Cody Lint, the kid who found your watch."

The phone was silent, and Mr. Provost didn't say anything.

I decided to continue. "Your wife gave us your cell phone number. We need your help."

Rachel yelled, "We have the statue, Mr. Provost. We found the bronze that was stolen from the Manitoba Council of Cree. But the two men who took it are trying to kill us—to keep everything a secret."

"Oh, my," he said.

The rough gravel road turned into smooth pavement, so we no longer had to shout to be heard. "We don't know anyone else who we can trust," I said, "or anyone who'll believe us."

"Have you called the police?" he asked.

"Yes," I said. "But one of the bad guys is Special Constable Brad Murphy."

"And he's chasing us in a police car!" Eric added. "We're on the river road, about five minutes south of town."

I glanced over my shoulder, but didn't see anyone. They were either dragging the spike belt from the road, or they had driven over it and ripped open their tires.

"Here's what you're going to do," Mr. Provost said. "I want you to drive straight to the MCC office in Pine Falls. I'm close by, and I'll meet you there."

"But these guys are dangerous," I said. "They have—"

"Don't worry," Mr. Provost said urgently. "Leave the rest to me. Just get yourselves to the MCC parking lot. Hurry!"

He disconnected before I could warn him about the guns.

Eric twisted around. "You better stomp on it, Rach. They're on us again, and I think they're catching up."

Rachel straightened out her leg and pushed hard on the gas pedal. The old truck rose up, enthusiastically barrelling down the highway. I didn't think we could outrun the high-performance police interceptor Brad was driving, but it sure felt like we were making good time. Then, just when I thought we had lost them for good, they were behind us again.

Rachel kept checking the rear-view mirror, and I knew she was worried.

"Just ignore them," I said, "and keep driving. You're doing great."

"I sure hope Mr. Provost knows what he's doing," she yelled.

When we got to Sultana, Rachel made a left turn, a right turn, and another left turn, and we continued down the highway to Pine Falls.

"If we're lucky," Eric said, "they'll waste time driving around Sultana looking for us. They'd never think we'd take Calvin's truck to the next town."

That seemed to be the case, because we drove west, almost all the way to Pine Falls, before Rachel gave us more bad news.

"Uh-oh," she said, using her thumb to point out the back window, "we've got trouble."

Eric and I spun around and looked behind the truck.

"That might not be them," I said, studying a vehicle in the distance that seemed to be rapidly gaining on us.

A second later, the car's emergency lights began to flash.

"Correction," Eric said, "that's absolutely Brad and Calvin."

Rachel ignored the police car chasing us and took us into the town of Pine Falls. We turned right on Cambrian Avenue and bounced into the parking lot of the Manitoba Council of Cree. The lot had spaces for ten cars on each side, but all the stalls were taken. Rachel stopped and left the truck right there in the middle of the parking lot and turned off the engine.

I noticed Mr. Provost's red suv parked at an awkward angle in the handicapped space.

Rachel noticed his car too. "Thank goodness," she said. "Mr. Provost is already here!"

Brad suddenly screeched to a halt behind us, blocking the entrance near the curb with his police cruiser. I'm sure he thought he was preventing our escape, but we had no intention of leaving. We were exactly where we were supposed to be.

The double doors of the building flew open, and Mr. Provost came out at a brisk walk. He was followed by a dozen other men and women with confused looks on their faces. I had the feeling he'd interrupted some sort of meeting. But that was okay with me. He quickly led everyone over to the truck—to the back of the truck.

We exited the cab and joined them around the tailgate.

Brad got out of his car and started shouting, "*Get back*! This is police business. Step away from that vehicle now!"

The passenger door of the police car also opened, and Creepy Calvin tried to get out. He teetered and then fell back into the seat, looking like he'd rather be in a hospital than in that parking lot.

A few people glanced in Brad's direction, but most ignored him, choosing instead to admire the giant bronze statue in the back of the truck.

Brad stomped closer and tried again. "*Get back!* This is a stolen vehicle. Those three kids are under arrest."

No one even looked at him that time.

A Cree elder in his seventies said, "I never thought we'd ever see him again." He reached over the side of the truck and touched the statue.

Mr. Provost pushed us closer to the elder and said, "Tell everyone where you found the statue."

We quickly spilled the story—how we found the statue, how we recovered it, and how we were abducted by Brad and Calvin. By the time we were done telling our crazy story, two more police cars and an ambulance arrived on the scene. Brad Murphy was cuffed with *real* handcuffs and shoved into the back of a cruiser, and a relieved-looking Calvin was hauled away by the paramedics.

Mr. Provost rubbed his hands together like he needed to warm them up. "I feel like a reporter on the crime beat again," he said, grinning. "This unsolved case has troubled me for a long time, and now you kids have finally set things right."

Everyone in the parking lot began clapping and cheering and crying.

Ten minutes later, the detachment commander, Superintendent Walker, arrived on the scene. He made us retell the entire story again. He took a few notes, but mostly he just listened.

When we were done, he said, "You boys were foolish to swim in the lake at night. That was beyond dangerous."

Eric and I nodded.

"And I hope you boys don't make a habit of driving trucks on the highway, either," he said.

"That was Rachel," Eric said, pointing at his sister. "She was the one who did all the driving."

"However," he continued, frowning at Eric's interruption, "all three of you were also extremely resourceful and courageous in escaping from those men. I would be pleased to have officers like you on the force someday."

We nodded again.

"And don't forget about the bronze," said Mr. Provost, who was still with us. "They recovered a statue that's been missing for a long time."

"Correct," he said. "I'm sure the Manitoba Council of Cree is pleased to have their memorial back."

"They're thrilled," Mr. Provost said.

Superintendent Walker cleared his throat. "I would also like to apologize for the behaviour of Brad Murphy. His actions were his own and should not taint your opinion of the RCMP or its members."

I wasn't sure what he meant by that, but it seemed like a good time for us to nod again.

CHAPTER 16

"LET ME SEE if I've got this right," Dad said. "In the last two days, Cody and his friends located and recovered a statue—one that's been missing for almost three decades. They solved a murder that the cops couldn't solve. And they helped capture the culprits and arrest them. Is that about it?"

I was eating pizza at the kitchen table, and Mom was trying her best to explain everything that had happened.

"No, dear," Mom said. "There's one more thing."

Dad groaned. "Don't tell me he's been elected mayor too."

"Worse!" she said. "I think Cody has a girlfriend."

It was my turn to groan now. "Mom!"

She explained how she'd seen Rachel hug me and kiss me on the cheek. That was true, of course, and the memory of it made me blush.

What happened was this. After the police took our official statements, they drove us back to Sultana and dropped us all off at my house. And that was when

Rachel hugged me. The shock of being suddenly squeezed by her sent my head spinning. But before I could say or do anything about that, she kissed my cheek.

Eric saw the kiss and cried, "Gross!"

Rachel ignored her brother and said, "Can we come over tomorrow?"

I nodded, still too stunned to speak.

Eric shook his head. "That kiss is going to make things awkward and bizarre for the rest of the summer."

"The summer is over, Eric," Rachel said. "And in case you haven't noticed, it was already a bizarre summer."

"As far as I'm concerned," I said to my friends, "this was the *best* summer ever."

Eric considered that for a few seconds, then nodded and said, "Best summer *ever!*"

"*Ever!*" Rachel echoed.

ACKNOWLEDGEMENTS

MASSIVE KUDOS AGAIN to everyone at Heritage House Publishing/Wandering Fox Books, for continuing to make the series look good on the inside and the outside.

AUTHOR
Q & A

Q *How long have you been writing?*

A I've been writing and experimenting with different genres of fiction for over twenty-five years.

Q *How did you end up writing for young people and specifically mysteries for young people?*

A When I first started writing, I wanted to write a book for adults, but I was nervous about the scope and size of a full-length paperback. So I decided instead to start with middle grade fiction, with its more manageable size of forty thousand words. After my first book was published, I found I really liked writing for that age group. Middle grade readers are sharp, ready for adventure, and appreciate humour. And two hundred pages gives me plenty of space to tell a complete story.

I've always enjoyed reading books of adventure and mystery, and now I have just as much fun writing those kinds of stories for young readers. I like the challenge of reverse engineering plots, sneaking in red herrings, and hitting the reader with a good twist now and then. And the more savvy middle graders become, the sneakier I have to be as a writer.

Q *What other kinds of writing do you do?*

A I also enjoy writing quirky short stories and submitting them to publishers. My dream is to one day see a story of mine in *Alfred Hitchcock Mystery Magazine*.

Q *Can you remember your first published piece? What was that like?*

A My first published work was a children's story printed in the United States. It wasn't a great piece, but being published (and paid royalties!) after collecting dozens of rejection letters was a real confidence boost for me. In fact, I think I was actually more excited about finally being published than I was about the story itself. That experience motivated and inspired me to continue to write and learn the craft.

Q *What advice do you have for young writers who want to get their stories published?*

A I have two pieces of advice.

First, don't listen to anyone who tells you to *only write what you know*. My advice is to *write about what you're interested in*. If that subject happens to be something you're already familiar with, then that's a bonus. But if you really want to write a story about ancient Egypt—because you saw *The Mummy* and you find the pyramids cool—go for it. That's exactly what I did in *History in the Faking*, by the way. I didn't know anything about hieroglyphics or long-dead pharaohs before I wrote the book, but the subject was so interesting to me, I researched the heck out of it, until I felt I could comfortably include the material in my story. The same is true for my other books. I don't know anything about jungles, the Second World War, or the Panama Canal, but I had fun writing about those things because the subject matter held my interest throughout the process. If I only wrote about things I know, I would either quickly get bored, or I would never get anything written, because I know very little.

And second, in order to get a story published, you have to finish the story. I know that sounds obvious, but a lot of great stories are never published, simply because the writers never finished them. So don't give up when your story is half done. Take your time, write a page a day, and keep plugging away. Even if you're not completely satisfied with the first draft—no writer is, trust me—you'll at least have something to edit. And after you revise that first draft, you'll suddenly have a second draft—one that'll make you eager to polish it a third time.

Q *How exactly do you go about writing a book? What's your process?*

A I usually let the spark of an idea (the premise) smoulder in my mind for a long time before I ever sit down to type a word. I won't even outline the plot, for fear that seeing those ideas on paper might somehow discourage me from further fleshing out the tale. Then, after I have a thorough understanding of the story in my head (strong beginning, exciting climax, satisfying conclusion), I'll start writing.

When I'm writing the first draft, I like to get the whole story finished before I start editing and rewriting. I don't stress about grammar, typos, or sentence structure, because I worry that if I spend too much time making every page perfect, I might get bogged down and discouraged from finishing the manuscript. After my rough first draft (usually very rough) is complete, I'll settle down and go over the work again and again—revising, editing, and fine-tuning.

Q   *What is your role as a writer once a book is finished?*

A   That's when the hard work really begins. For a book to be successful—especially in Canada—a writer has to be an active participant in marketing and promoting their work. I often visit schools and do readings and presentations. I maintain my website and Facebook pages. And I email as many bookstores and libraries as I can, trying to spread the word when a new title is available.

Q   *In this book, we see the typical sites of a small town: golf course, pathways, restaurants, back yards, community halls. Do you make the story fit a specific community, or do you create sites that fit the story?*

A   The town of Sultana is fictional, but it is typical of many small towns in eastern Manitoba. I suppose I could have used any one of those real communities for the setting, but I'm always nervous about messing up the details and offending someone from an actual town. *"Hey, dummy, Pine Street isn't next to Birch Street."* That kind of thing. But by inventing my own community—Sultana in this case—I can put the river exactly where I need it, I can place the streets where I want them, and I can locate businesses where they make the most sense.

Q *What kind of resources did you use to research and write this book?*

A My office is next to the Lac du Bonnet Regional Library, so that's always a great place to hang out and look things up in books. But I'm also a big fan of computer search engines. It's incredibly convenient to open Google, enter a question—HOW MUCH DOES A GOLF BALL WEIGH?—and instantly get an answer (forty-six grams, in case you're curious).

Q *Do you have any stories about the challenges you faced in writing this book?*

A The biggest challenge I faced in writing *In Too Deep* was deciding if Cody and Eric should use snorkelling gear or scuba diving equipment when they went into the lake looking for golf balls. In my first draft, I had the boys using scuba equipment, but the more I thought about it, the less realistic and plausible that seemed. I mean, it's not unheard of for teens to scuba dive, but I felt I wasn't playing fair with readers, suddenly having the boys qualified to use regulators and air tanks. Anyway, I rewrote the scenes at Smoke Lake, replacing scuba diving with snorkelling.

Q *How do you grow and develop the characters of the three friends in each book?*

A In *History in the Faking* (the first book of the Shenanigans series), I wanted to quickly demonstrate that Cody, Eric, and Rachel had unique personalities. But one of the great things about a series is that I could also take my time (in subsequent books) and really explore a character's development. For example, when we first met Cody he was a nervous kid, worrying about the silliest things (gravity disappearing, the sun burning out, etc.). He's still appropriately cautious in this story, but he's no longer anxious about every challenge he and his friends face. Rachel has also grown as a character. She's still consistently intelligent, but she's also gotten bolder and braver with each book. But then there's Eric. Readers often tell me that he's a favourite character, so I have fun keeping Eric lazy, silly, hungry, and a real smarty pants.

Q *Will there be a sixth book in the Shenanigans series?*

A I still have plenty of ideas for mischief for Cody and his friends, so I'll keep documenting their shenanigans as long as readers continue to enjoy the books.

THE SHENANIGANS SERIES

978-1-77203-008-2, $9.95

978-1-77203-058-7, $9.95

978-1-77203-067-9, $9.95

978-1-77203-097-6, $9.95

Available where all fine books are sold.

heritagehouse.ca

ABOUT the AUTHOR

ANDREAS OERTEL was born in Germany and has lived most of his life in eastern Manitoba. He is the author of the critically acclaimed Shenanigans series, which has been nominated for several awards, including the Silver Birch Award, the Manitoba Young Readers Choice Award, and the New York State Reading Association Charlotte Award. He has a lifelong passion for archaeology, history, and writing for young people. Learn more at andreasoertel.com.